Head Over Heels

B Crowhurst

Copyright © 2023 by B Crowhurst

Cover design by B Crowhurst

Image rights obtained from Deposit Photos

All rights reserved.

No portion of this book may be reproduced in any form without written permission from the publisher or author, except as permitted by U.S. copyright law.

I would like to dedicate this book to all mothers, everywhere.

Motherhood is tough, but it's also wonderful.

Always remember who you were before you were *Mum* and that you are enough.

Chapter One

Amanda

"I swear to God, Ronan, if you don't get your backside in this car for school in the next thirty seconds, you will not be going to rugby on Saturday and you can kiss goodbye to your PlayStation this week."

I hang up the phone and toss it on the front seat. This is what my life has become, phoning and texting my children in the vague hope they might listen to me. Ruby fortunately is already sat in the backseat as I impatiently rev the engine and drum my fingernails on the steering wheel. Eventually, Ronan emerges from the house lazily, with his backpack slung over one shoulder and his hair gelled to perfection. He even has the audacity to yawn as he casually makes his way down the driveway to the car. *You do not want to push my buttons today, sunshine.*

"Have you seen the time?" I bark at him the second he opens the car door and slides in next to his sister. Ronan just shrugs and looks out the window.

"Do you really want your third late mark in as many days? It's the first week of term, Ronan, this year is important. You're going to be choosing your GCSEs."

Ronan takes the opportunity to roll his eyes as I briefly pause for breath but still says nothing. I can't actually remember the last time I heard him do anything other than grunt.

"Not to mention, work is going to fire my arse soon if you don't stop making me late." I have no idea why I'm ranting at him like this. It won't change anything; I may as well be shouting into an empty car for all the good it'll do me.

Just to further prove my point and enrage me more, Ronan picks up his headphones and puts them on. I floor the accelerator in frustration and zoom in and out of the traffic trying to make up the lost time. As we reach the turning for the school, I pull up across the road from the gate.

"Mum?" Ruby asks as she grabs her bag.

"Yes?" I look at her in the rear-view mirror as I touch up my lipstick for work.

"Can I have some more lunch money?"

"Well, what happened to the week's worth I gave you two days ago?" I snap back. *These guys are really testing my patience this morning.*

Ruby just shrugs at me in the mirror in that sulky way that teenagers do.

"Does nobody have any response other than a shrug today?" I ask myself, more than anyone.

Ronan reaches for the door handle and steps out the car without so much as a backward glance. "Laters" he mumbles over his shoulder before slamming the door so hard he makes the car shake. *Count to ten, Amanda. You're the adult.* I try to remind myself what I had only been reading in my 'Modern Parenting' book the previous night. *What bollocks. Moody, ungrateful little shits.* I take a deep breath, so I don't completely lose my mind before reaching for my purse. I calmly hand Ruby a five-pound note. "Is this enough?"

Ruby nods and reaches forward to pocket the money. "Love you Mum." She kisses my cheek quick so none of her friends see and gets out the car. Just like that, most of my anger dissipates into nothing and I sigh as I pull back out into the traffic.

How is it possible to absolutely love the bones of them and know that I would lay my life down for them but at the same time, they can piss me off faster than anything else on Earth? Parenting is a funny thing. No one ever said it would be easy, but my God, raising twins alone from the age of four has been a hell of a ride. Like trying to hold on to some out-of-control rodeo bull with your hands tied behind your back and someone throwing balled up socks at your head…or something equally as impossible.

Ten years I have been muddling through this single parenting nightmare. I keep waiting for the 'better' that everyone talks about, but I've come to the conclusion that it's a myth, much like the ends of rainbows. You never actually get there.

I realise that I've been musing the absurdity of parenthood in my head so long that I'm already at work and for once with three minutes to spare. *Go me.* I only work part-time as a receptionist at the local hotel but it keeps us comfortable enough and it fits for now.

I smooth out my uniform as I step out of the car. It consists of a grey skirt and jacket, white blouse and red heels to match the red neckerchief that sits ruffled at my chest. Whoever came up with this outfit clearly was not well endowed because if they were, they would realise how impractical it is to not be able to see your own feet over all the scarlet ruffles. Being curvy is both a blessing and a curse, depending on what mood I'm in.

I maximise my three spare minutes to make a hot cup of coffee to take with me to reception and set myself up for the day. Every morning I have to alter the height of the seat. *I'm convinced they employ giants to work the night shift.*

With my steaming coffee, freshly applied red lipstick and correctly adjusted chair, I feel ready to take on the world. For all of five minutes that is, until the phone rings with a complaint and the day turns to shit.

By the time 3pm rolls around, I've had enough for the day. I've been shouted at more times than I can count, dealt with two sets of lost luggage and juggled a fire drill. To top it all off, I managed to spill the soup I had for lunch down my blouse and have to keep yanking my jacket further across my chest despite its already strained efforts to cover me. *What a day.*

While I'm packing up my things, my phone rings in my handbag.

"Hello?" I answer, tucking the phone under my chin so I can carry on getting ready to leave and pick up the kids.

"Hello, is that Miss Wells?"

"Yes, speaking,"

"Hello Miss Wells, it's Mrs Bates, the school secretary. I'm afraid there's been an incident. Please can you come straight to the Headmaster's office when you come to collect the children?"

"Oh my God, are they ok?" I ask hurriedly as I grab my car keys and rush out the door.

"Yes, they're fine, please don't worry," she tries to reassure me.

My initial panic subsides and switches to suspicion. "What have they done?"

"I think it's best you just come in and Mr Woodgate can explain."

I stuff the phone back in my bag as I reach the car and drive to the school like a woman possessed, muttering the whole way about various ways in which I'm going to murder the twins when I get hold of them. *It's the first week of term! How am I being hauled into the Head's office already? A brand new one at that!* We had a letter at the end of last year to explain that due to the school's failing results they were bringing in a new 'Executive Head' to help bring the school up to scratch. *Whatever one of those is.*

When I arrive at the school, I push my way through the oncoming crowd of kids all exiting the premises. Most of them don't even attempt to move out of my way. A couple of the older boys wolf whistle as I march through the grounds in my red heels. I resist the urge to flip them the bird as it dawns on me that I have no clue where the Headmaster's office even is. Ruby and Ronan never let me get closer than dropping them across the road from the gate because apparently, I'm 'too embarrassing' to be seen with. *This day just gets better and better.*

Thankfully when I arrive through the double doors at the main entrance, I'm greeted by the receptionist I spoke to on the phone who escorts me down a short corridor to Mr Woodgate's office. She knocks gently and a deep voice from inside instructs me to "come in". The receptionist smiles sympathetically at me before retreating back to where she came from. *Oh Lord, what am I walking into?* I take a deep breath and enter the room.

I'm greeted by the sight of an outrageously handsome man in a dark suit, sitting behind a large mahogany desk. *Ok, he is not at all what I was expecting.* I have no idea what I was expecting, but he is not it. He has dark hair with a smattering of silver at his temples and a strong jaw. If I had to guess, I'd say he was somewhere in his mid forties but I suck at aging people. He's rugged and manly with a dark, short beard but also sleek and intelligent looking, wearing a pair of square framed reading glasses that he takes off as I enter. The twins are sat either side of his office looking suitably sullen. Ronan is nursing a fat lip with an ice pack and his eye is a shocking shade of purple. Ruby is red and puffy where she has clearly been crying and her hair is matted and wild. *Jesus Christ, my kids are feral.*

"Hello Miss Wells, I'm Mr Woodgate. I don't believe I've had the pleasure." The Headmaster's deep velvety voice resonates round his office as he comes round from behind his desk to shake my hand.

I clumsily take his hand, my mind reeling at how embarrassing and awkward this whole scenario is. He gestures for me to take a seat in the empty chair in front of his desk between the twins. As I sit down, I give each of them a murderous glare, the one that only mothers can produce before I look up at Mr Woodgate with the best poker face I can manage. It's at that moment I remember the stain down the front of my blouse and nervously try to pull my jacket across to hide it. *What am I so nervous about? It's not me who's in trouble.*

Mr Woodgate stands in front of his desk and leans back against it slightly causing his shirt to strain across his chest. *Now is not the time Amanda.* My train of thought could not be any less appropriate right now.

"As I'm sure you've gathered Miss Wells, there was an incident this afternoon that has landed Ronan and Ruby in rather a lot of trouble." I nod silently waiting for him to continue.

"Ronan, would you like to explain to your mum what happened?"

Ronan shrugs his shoulders and looks at the floor.

"No, Mr Woodgate is the appropriate response." He doesn't shout but his tone is authoritative and makes all three of us snap to attention. His manner is commanding but somehow not threatening.

"No, Mr Woodgate," Ronan mumbles before continuing to stare at his shoes.

"Very well." Mr Woodgate folds his arms across his chest and looks directly at me. "It would seem there was some upset between Ruby and some of her peers which resulted in Ruby and another girl pulling fistfuls of each other's hair out."

I gasp in response and look at Ruby. I expect these kinds of physical reactions from Ronan, he's always been impulsive, but I'm shocked by Ruby.

"She started it though Mum." Ruby sobs and throws her head in to her hands.

"Ruby, why don't you tell us in your own words what happened." Mr Woodgate prompts gently. He's such a unique blend of stern and empathetic.

Ruby sniffles and looks up at us both in turn. "Amber-May started laughing at me for ordering dessert at lunch. She was saying that it's no wonder I'm fat and that I should care more about my figure. They were all laughing and making pig noises. Then one of the other girls said I should go and make myself sick before it was too late. She leaned over my tray and spat in my food...so I grabbed her by the hair and pushed her backwards." Ruby barely manages to finish the last sentence before she begins sobbing again.

Mr Woodgate passes Ruby a tissue as my heart breaks for my daughter. *How can girls be so cruel to each other? How dare they make her feel bad about herself like that?* I reach for Ruby and hold her in my arms as she continues to cry uncontrollably.

"I'm sorry Mum, I shouldn't have got into a fight." She wails into my suit jacket as a huge wet patch creeps across it to go with the lunch stain on my blouse.

"Oh, sweetheart," I murmur as I stroke her hair.

Mr Woodgate clears his throat and returns behind his desk to sit in his chair. "I can assure you Miss Wells that the other girls have been dealt with accordingly. We do not tolerate that kind of bullying and body shaming in this school. However, I'm sure you can appreciate that I also cannot allow physical retaliations either." He looks at me with concern, clearly trying to gauge what sort of reaction I'm going to give.

"No, I understand that." I assure him before turning to my daughter who is regaining a little composure. "Ruby, we will talk about what they said to you later but how could you have handled that better?" I ask her. I've always tried to encourage them both to think for themselves.

Ruby opens her mouth to respond but Ronan interrupts before she can say anything.

"She should have smashed her head on the damn table!" Ronan scoffs. "Stuck up brat had it coming!"

I don't know whether I want to die of embarrassment at his words or high-five him for caring so much about his sister, (not that he would ever admit that's what this was, in a million years.) I feel my cheeks flush. I'm not sure how to handle this situation in front of Mr Woodgate. Poor Ruby is distraught, Ronan is like some sort of misguided vigilante, and I'm supposed to be the responsible parent who knows what to do in this situation. The fact that the new Headmaster is insanely good looking, isn't helping matters at all. It's just further frying my already overwhelmed brain. *Fuck adulting.*

Mr Woodgate doesn't respond to Ronan's harsh words, he simply steeples his fingers under his chin and ever so subtly raises an eyebrow at me as if waiting and watching for my response. Something deep inside me stirs at his expression but now is not the time to explore that particular, wildly unfamiliar feeling. So instead, I look at Ronan.

"And what was your part in all this?" I ask him sharply, choosing to ignore what he just said for the time being. *One thing at a time.* "I swear to God Ronan, if I find out you hit a girl..."

Ronan snaps his head up and glares at me as he interrupts me. "No of course not! Who do you think I am?

Dad?" *Ouch*. Ruby flinches at Ronan's mention of their father and Mr Woodgate's brow briefly furrows into a frown but is quickly returns to a mask of calm.

"Amber-May's boyfriend got involved and started saying stuff about Ruby too, so I smacked him in the face." Ronan mumbles as he goes back to looking at his shoes.

"Ronan" I groan. He's always been the type to act first and think later.

"What? I don't like people saying stuff about Ruby. They need to shut up and mind their own business." Ronan adds sulkily. I notice him wince as he talks, reopening the gash on his lip.

"Whilst your intentions are noble Ronan, I cannot tolerate acts of physical violence. You do understand that, right?" Mr Woodgate asks calmly.

"Whatever."

"Given each of your previous behaviour records and the circumstances of today's events, I will be giving Ruby a written warning and we will work closely with you to resolve this situation with the other girls. Ronan, you will be serving detention after school with me for the next three days. Does that sound fair?" Mr Woodgate looks at each of the twins in turn but neither of them speaks.

"Yes, I think so." I answer for them. "Thank you, Mr Woodgate, I'm sorry for the inconvenience."

He gives me a warm smile that sends my stomach into a frenzy of somersaults. "Not at all." His eyes linger for a second on my face as he stands to show us out.

"Now, let's let your mum get home for a well-deserved rest, shall we? It must be tiring jetting off from place to place."

Ronan almost smiles and Ruby sniggers before I hit her on the arm playfully to stop her. "Oh, I'm not a flight attendant. It's this silly uniform they make us wear. I'm a receptionist at The Hammond Hotel." I explain. *People always think I'm a flight attendant.*

"Oh, I see. My mistake. Well, all the same I'm sure you've had a long day. Good evening, Miss Wells."

He holds his hand out for me to shake it as he opens the door. "I hope to see you again at the parent's meeting later this week."

I nod and shake his hand, holding my breath so as not to breathe in his aftershave, it might just tip me over the edge.

As we walk away down the corridor, I can hear my heels clicking on the hard floor.

"I'll see you tomorrow in detention." Mr Woodgate calls out after us to Ronan, who vaguely waves his hand in the air in acknowledgement.

"Home you two, now." I mutter under my breath. *God, give me strength.*

Chapter Two

Tyler

What the fuck is wrong with me? I look and feel like shit this morning. I barely slept last night going over yesterday's events in my head over and over again. Never in all my years in education have I *ever* been remotely attracted to a parent. Intimate relationships with parents isn't strictly breaking any rules but it's not exactly encouraged either. Many would consider it a conflict of interest.

I look in the mirror and splash more cold water on my face in the hopes of looking less tired, but it's not working. *Get it together, Tyler.* Every time I closed my eyes last night, all I saw was those full red lips and that curvy figure in my mind. Not to mention those legs in those red heels. *Fuck, those legs.* Amanda Wells was not at all what I had expected to walk into my office, and it caught me off guard completely. It's not a feeling I'm used to, I'm used to being in control. That's how I like it.

I grab my briefcase and head out the door as I continue to replay the events in my mind for the hundredth time. *What on earth was I thinking making Ronan come to detention in my office for the next three days?* Not only do I not have time for that, but it also means I will be seeing Amanda Wells again for the next three afternoons when she collects him. *Damn it.* Not to mention the fact that I then felt the need to personally remind her to come to the meeting on Friday. The last thing I need when I'm speaking publicly for the first time in my new role is to be distracted by her pouty lips and plunging cleavage. *Fuck it, I'm screwed. Come on Tyler. You're better than this. You're a professional, who absolutely cannot and will not give in to the primal urges of your dick, no matter how badly you want to.* This is the shit I keep telling myself all the way to work.

On my arrival, Pam is in the reception office ready and waiting with my coffee as seems to be the norm. I've never once asked her to make coffee but she does it as part of her morning routine. It's very early days at this new school but so far everyone has been very welcoming. It's tough in this job, moving from school to school. I just build a school up and get it to a point where it's thriving and then I have to move on to the next one. That's the whole point of it though I guess.

"Good morning, Mr Woodgate." Pam chirps as she follows me into my office, no doubt to update me on the upcoming events of the day.

"Pam, please, you can call me Tyler when the students aren't around." I put my briefcase down on my desk and switch the computer on.

"Sorry Mr Woodgate, will do," she says absentmindedly. She's too busy shuffling bits of paper and adding them to my growing pile of things to read on my desk. "So today you've got the meeting with the Chair of Governors at 11am and then you are pencilled in to sit in on the Key Stage 3 planning meeting this afternoon."

I nod as Pam continues to put newsletters and meeting minutes on my desk.

"Oh, and don't forget you have a webinar at three thirty."

"Cancel that for me please, Pam and send my apologies. I've got Ronan Wells coming to do detention."

Pam stops what she's doing and frowns at me. "Can't someone else do that for you? Surely you've got more important issues than babysitting?"

The look on my face turns Pam's cheeks scarlet red. "There is a student who is having a tough time and working through some issues. What could be more important than that?" I ask sternly.

"Yes of course, sorry Mr Woodgate. I'll cancel the webinar." She says, scurrying out of my office and closing the door behind her.

I lean back in my chair and let out a sigh. Visions of Amanda sat in the chair opposite my desk fill my mind. The thought of her long legs crossed with those shiny red heels have me needing to rearrange myself in my suit. *It's going to be a long day.*

• • • ● ● ● ● ● • • •

As it happens, the day ends up flying by and before I know it there's a knock on the door.

"Come in." I call without looking up from my computer.

A sulky looking Ronan shuffles into my office and shuts the door. He doesn't look at me, his eyes stay firmly fixed on the floor.

"Good afternoon, Ronan, how was your day?" I ask with a smile, giving him my full attention. I want to know why this kid is so angry at the world.

"Fine," he mumbles.

"Good, well please take a seat. Do you have homework you can be doing? May as well make good use of the time." I suggest.

Ronan nods and opens his backpack up on my desk, producing a stack of books. He silently pulls up a chair and gets to work across the desk from me, not looking at me once.

I'm about to quiz him on his day when my office phone rings. For the next twenty minutes I'm stuck on a call that I'm unable to wrap up. I can see that Ronan is sketching but I can't see what it is from here. He's in deep concentration and for the first time since meeting him, his face looks stress-free. He isn't scowling, he's completely lost in what he's doing.

Eventually I'm able to hang up the phone. "Is that art homework Ronan?" I ask, genuinely interested.

"Yeah, it's my art journal," he mumbles.

"What's the assignment?"

"Just to draw whatever we feel like and stuff, whenever we want." Ronan shrugs; his usual response, and continues to sketch.

"Mind if I take a look?"

Ronan slides the sketch book across the desk to me and I start to scan through the pages. *This kid has some serious talent*. I fan through numerous detailed still-life sketches before coming across a picture of his sister, Ruby. She's looking to the side and laughing. It really is an impressive drawing by anyone's standards, let alone a fourteen-year-old boy.

"These are wonderful Ronan. You have a real talent."

He half-smiles and mumbles, "Thanks."

I turn the page and the next sketch takes me breath away. It's a picture of Amanda with tears streaming down her face. The drawing is flawless, such a true likeness, although it angers me to see her so sad.

"This one of your mother..." I start to say.

"Yeah forget that one, I shouldn't have drawn it. She'll kill me if she knows it's in here."

"Tell me about it." I run my fingers over the pencil lines as I listen.

"Mum gets sad sometimes. Well, a lot actually. She thinks that just because she waits for us to go to bed before she cries that we don't know about it."

An uncomfortable pain sits heavily on my chest. "What makes her sad, Ronan?"

"It used to be my dad. He used to hit her and stuff but after he left, I think it's just because she gets lonely." He pauses for a second before adding, "Me and Ruby aren't easy either."

This kid is carrying so much on his young shoulders, it's no wonder he's so troubled and angry all the time. The urge to help him and his heartbreakingly beautiful mother is overwhelming. It's only then that I realise my fists have balled at my sides listening to him. I relax them and clear my throat. I need to keep level-headed about all of this. I can't let my attraction to this woman cloud my judgement and professionalism.

Ronan and I pass the remainder of his detention chatting. He's actually a lovely boy once he opens up and starts talking. He has so much potential; all he needs is the right guidance through his emotional troubles.

Right on cue, at five o'clock I hear the distinct sound of high heels coming up the corridor. The sound alone has my cock twitching. *God dammit.* A soft knock at the door signals her arrival.

"Good afternoon, Miss Wells." I greet her with a smile from behind my desk, not wanting to stand up in case it's obvious just how pleased I am to see her.

"Hello Mr Woodgate, I hope Ronan has behaved himself?" she asks as if she's worried that her son has inconvenienced me in some way.

Ronan rolls his eyes and shuts down instantly. The chatty, care-free Ronan from five minutes ago has gone, only to be replaced with the sulky, moody version that the world mostly sees. *Interesting.*

"He's been excellent company as it goes and he's produced some outstanding homework while he's been here." I say in the hopes of boosting his confidence a little.

"Oh, that's good to hear. Well done, darling," she smiles at him with obvious love and pride but Ronan doesn't see as he's gone back to looking at the floor. "Well, we won't take up any more of your time, I'm sure you're a very busy man." She says hurriedly as she starts scooping up Ronan's stuff.

"I'll never be too busy for you," I reply without thinking. "that's my job." I add quickly.

Amanda stops what she's doing and looks directly at me. She only pauses for the briefest of moments but she almost floors me. She really is absolutely stunning.

"Thank you." Her hair is down today and flows around her shoulders in auburn waves. She has the same uniform on as yesterday except today's heels are black and grey pinstripe with a red strap. I've never taken notice of a woman's shoes before but she wears hers so well. They're like her signature piece, those and the matching red lipstick that I just want to run my tongue along and…

"Mr Woodgate?" The sound of Amanda's voice snaps me out of my completely inappropriate daydream. I bring my eyes back up to her face, not realising they had briefly wandered south to her legs in those heels.

Her expression is a cross between embarrassment and amusement. "We'll see you tomorrow then." She nods before opening my door.

"Tomorrow." I repeat as I listen to the sound of her clicking down the corridor away from my office. *I am so royally fucked.*

• • • ● ● • ● • • •

Ronan's second detention is proving to be even more enlightening than the first. I took the time to speak with his teachers today to learn more about him and he really does seem to be a very promising young man indeed, if he could only control his temper and mood swings. I've always been drawn to the misunderstood students. Something in me gets a kick out of getting through to them.

Ronan brings an essay with him to do and sits quietly at my desk writing while I send a bunch of emails I've been trying to get around to all day.

"Mr Woodgate?" Ronan speaks first, to my surprise.

"Yes?"

"Can I ask you something?" he shifts awkwardly in his seat.

"Of course, Ronan, you can always ask me anything."

"Do you think that bad people stay bad forever, or do you think they can change?" Ronan taps his pencil on the desk, nervously waiting for my response. My answer to this question clearly means a lot to him, so I choose my words carefully.

"I think everyone is capable of change, if they really want to. And I'm not sure if I believe anyone is truly bad. What do you think?"

Ronan's shoulders visibly relax at my answer. "I hope so. Not everyone who's bad does it on purpose," he says, thoughtfully.

"Why do you ask? Do you know someone who wants to change?" I try to make it so the question is not directly about him in the hopes he will keep opening up to me.

"Me, I do. I don't mean to be a shit…er, I mean difficult. I just get so…angry," he admits.

I switch my computer screen off so he knows he has my undivided attention and lean forward slightly in my chair. "What makes you think you're bad Ronan? There's nothing wrong with feeling angry from time to time, it's perfectly normal. It's how you deal with it that counts."

Ronan nods in understanding. "I want to do better. I want to make them proud," he whispers sadly.

"Who? Your mum and Ruby?" I ask.

Ronan nods again and wipes his eyes with his sleeve, trying to disguise the fact that he's getting upset. I don't embarrass him by commenting on it.

"I think they're already proud. You're a bright young man Ronan. I've got some things I'd like you to try to help you manage some of these feelings. How does that sound?"

"I make Mum sad; I don't mean to. I don't know why I do it. I'm meant to look after her now. I'm the man of the house, or whatever."

I reach across to pat Ronan's arm. My own feelings of anger are simmering under the surface. I'm not angry at Ronan, he's just a confused kid but I am angry at the thought of what has happened and continues to happen in their lives. I've tried so hard to remain impartial but something about Amanda and her children draws me in despite my better judgement.

"Ronan, that's a big responsibility you've given yourself there. No one expects that of you, least of all your mum, I'm sure. I bet all she really wants is for you to be happy, just like you want for her."

Ronan nods and gives me half a smile.

"I've got some ideas for some ways we can work together to make things better, what do you say?" Behind me I hear someone clear their throat.

I had been so engrossed in my conversation with Ronan that I hadn't heard the tell-tale sound of Amanda's heels coming along the corridor. She's standing in my office doorway in her pristine uniform. Today's shoes are black with red heels that match her lipstick as always. Her hair is up with a few loose tendrils framing her face. She literally takes my breath away each time I see her.

"Sorry to interrupt," she says softly. "I'm a few minutes early. Traffic was good today."

"No, that's fine. Ronan and I were just discussing a few things. Were you standing there long?" I ask, trying to sound casual but frantically rewinding the conversation in my head to see if I said anything that makes me sound like an idiot.

"Just a moment." She smiles at me and my whole body reacts in ways I wish it wouldn't.

"I have the behaviour report written up from the incident the other day. I wondered if you could read and sign it for me, please?" I ask, as I reach for the papers in my top drawer.

"Yes of course, Ronan why don't you go and wait in the car?" She hands Ronan the keys who is only too happy to be let out of detention early. Before he leaves the room, he turns back to me and mumbles.

"Thanks Mr Woodgate."

As soon as Ronan leaves the room and his footsteps trail off down the corridor, the atmosphere shifts instantly and the air seems to crackle with electricity. Amanda takes a seat in the chair opposite my desk and crosses her long legs, flashing me the red sole of her shoe. I swallow hard and slide the report across the desk to her, taking a seat. It's safer if I stay on the opposite side. She takes the piece of paper and starts to silently read. I can't help but notice the way her forehead wrinkles slightly when she concentrates and her lips part ever so subtly. Eventually she finishes reading and looks up at me.

"This all seems fair and accurate." She smiles and glances around my desk for a pen.

I hand her one from my jacket pocket and she takes it from me without breaking eye contact.

"Thank you, Mr Woodgate."

I don't know if she intended that to be the most seductive goddamn thing I ever heard or if it was said in innocence but *fuck*. All I can think about is how good she would look spread across my desk in nothing but those heels.

Amanda finishes signing the paperwork and leaves the pen on my desk as she stands. She makes her way to the door before looking back at me over her shoulder and smiling.

"Goodnight."

I'm so getting fired and going to hell.

Chapter Three

Amanda

Today has been a shit show. Just when I think things are starting to settle a little and I might finally be getting the hang of life, I have a day like today. First my alarm didn't go off so we overslept, then the car took ages to start. I got a tongue-lashing from a customer at work and then less than two minutes ago as I was sipping my first coffee of the day, *mid-afternoon*, when I realised that Ruby has the dentist but Ronan will be in his last detention. *Crap.*

I decide to do what I always do in a crisis and call my sister, Chloe. She's got this adulting shit down to a tee and always seems to have everything under control, unlike me.

• • • ● • ● • • •

"Thanks for getting Ronan." I say to Chloe later that evening as I stir the casserole.

"No problem, I can see what you mean now about that Mr Bigwood. He is dreamy." My sister wiggles her eyebrows as she sips her tea.

"Ssh keep your voice down!" I whisper loudly, afraid one of the kids might hear her. "And his name is Mr Woodgate."

"Bigwood is more fitting I'd say." Chloe snorts and laughs.

I slap Chloe on the arm for her inappropriate remarks. I made the mistake of mentioning how insanely hot he is on the phone earlier. Before I can change the subject, she continues.

"And if I'm not mistaken, he looked rather disappointed that I wasn't you."

"What? Don't be daft." I shrug and go back to stirring.

"I would have been offended if I wasn't so freaking excited for you!" she comes over to where I'm standing and nudges me playfully.

"Excited about what? Are you high?" I turn to Chloe to see her grinning like a Cheshire cat.

"You know, for you to finally see some action, and from the Headmaster no less! So damn hot," she swoons.

I shush her again and swat her with my tea towel. "You've officially lost your mind."

"Oh, come on, like you haven't thought long and *hard* about him bending you over his desk and teaching you a lesson."

I gasp and laugh out loud. My sister has never been one to hold back or mince her words. I stop and sigh, thinking about what she's saying.

"Even if that were true," I raise an eyebrow at her to let her know that it is, "parent teacher relationships are not exactly the done thing."

"All the more reason to go for it, I say," she says with a wink. Chloe always bent the rules as a kid, then outright ignored them as a teen. "Listen, I know what I saw today. That man deflated like a balloon after a birthday party when I walked in instead of you. No one is going to bring happiness to you Mandy, you've got to go grab it by the bollocks and drag it kicking and screaming to you."

Chloe puts her arm around my shoulders and squeezes. That was her version of a pep talk. I smile at her letting her words sink in. *Maybe she has a point.*

"Now how long is this casserole going to take? I'm starving."

• • • ● ● • ● • • •

Chloe goes home after dinner and the kids disappear off up to their rooms so I take the opportunity to pour myself a glass of wine before starting on the mountain of washing up. As soon as I put my hands in the water, my phone starts to ring. I manage to dry my hands and reach for it by the third ring but I don't recognise the number.

"Hello?" I answer, resting the phone on my shoulder under my chin so I can continue with the dishes.

"Hello Miss Wells, it's Mr Woodgate."

My stomach instantly flutters at the unexpected sound of his voice. I almost drop the phone in the soapy water. *Why is he calling me?*

"Oh hello, is everything alright?" I somehow manage to sound less flustered than I feel.

"Yes, I was just calling to make sure everything is ok as I didn't see you at pick up today for Ronan. I was hoping to speak with you about some options going forward."

"Sorry about that, I had to take Ruby to the dentist so my sister offered to step in. You didn't need to phone out of hours, I'm sure you're a busy man. I can come in on Monday if you like?" *Stop rambling Amanda.*

"Well, I'm just on my way home now and thought I'd drop the paperwork to you so I can explain it. Then you've got the weekend to think and read it over. Only if that's alright of course."

"Yes of course," I blurt out without thinking. "That really is very nice of you, there's no need to inconvenience yourself on our account though."

"It's no trouble at all. I'll see you shortly," he says before hanging up.

Shit! He's coming here, like here, to my house. I look at myself in the reflection of the window and remember I'm wearing a sweatshirt and leggings with absolutely no make-up on. I sprint up the stairs and run in to the bathroom to brush my teeth and apply some light make-up. My hair is a lost cause so I just sweep it up into a pile on top of my head. *That will have to do.* Just as I'm about to change my outfit I hear a knock at the door. *Damn it.*

Before answering the door, I take a few deep breaths so I don't sound like I've just been sprinting round the house like a mad woman. A blast of cold air enters the house when I open the door and Mr Woodgate turns to me with a smile. He's wearing a dark coat over his suit with a navy scarf wound round his neck. The autumn wind has done wonderful things to his hair and he somehow seems taller now that he's in my small doorway.

"Hello," he greets me, taking his hands out of his pockets.

"Hi," I reply, feeling awkward. *I have no idea what the appropriate thing is to say or do in this situation.* I've never had a hotter than hell Headmaster in my house before. I open the door wider and gesture for him to come inside.

As soon as he's in the small confines of my hallway his presence is everywhere. He smells incredible and he looks even better up this close. The air crackles with sexual tension but I still can't tell if he notices it too or if it's all in my head.

"Can I get you a drink? I'm about to put the kettle on." I ask, just for something to say.

"A coffee would be lovely actually." He follows me through the narrow hallway to the kitchen and stands at the breakfast bar as I fill the kettle.

I busy myself with making drinks so I don't have to look at him. Seeing him in my house is really surreal.

"I've had some very insightful conversations with Ronan these past few days. He really is an intelligent and talented young man." Mr Woodgate says as he takes out an envelope full of papers from inside his coat.

"Thank you, he's a good boy really." I sigh, stirring the coffee. "He just let's his emotions get the better of him."

"I quite agree, which is why I think he could benefit from some sessions with the school counsellor." He smiles and takes the coffee I pass him. "I have the permission forms here if you think it's something Ronan could benefit from and would engage with."

Taking the paperwork, I skim read the pages to see what it involves as I finish making the coffee.

"Please take all the time you need to think about it." Mr Woodgate adds, making me realise I haven't actually responded to what he said.

"I think this would be great for him, thank you Mr Woodgate." I say, handing him his coffee and searching under a pile of magazines for a pen to sign with.

He hands me one from inside his jacket pocket. "Please, call me Tyler. We're not in school now."

My eyes snap up to his, surprised by his request. "That's not entirely appropriate, is it?"

"The best things in life often aren't." He says slowly with such intensity that I can't look away. It's not until he reaches over and straightens my coffee mug that I realise it must have been tilting as I was staring at him. *Shit, snap out of it, Amanda.*

He smiles at me sexily and takes a sip of coffee but still doesn't break eye contact.

Ronan and Ruby walk into the kitchen behind me making me jump, almost spilling my coffee for the second time tonight.

"Hi Mr Woodgate, what are you doing here?" Ruby asks casually as she helps herself to a carton of juice from the fridge.

"Hello Ruby, Ronan. I'm just here to give some paperwork to your mum. I missed her at pick-up." He looks back at me as he finishes his last sentence. *Is he actually flirting with me or have I completely lost my mind at last?*

Ruby shrugs, seemingly satisfied with the answer and I swear Ronan is almost smiling. *What is happening right now?* Ronan seems to respond so well to Mr Woodgate, *Tyler*.

"Why are you drinking coffee?" Ruby suddenly asks, studying me. "You never drink coffee this late."

"Yes, I do," I argue back, knowing full well she's right. *Damn smart kids.*

"And why have you put make-up on? You didn't have any on at dinner."

I feel my cheeks heat with embarrassment. *I can't believe she's calling me out in front of Mr Woodgate, Tyler, whatever!*

I glance across and see him attempt to hide a smile behind his coffee mug as he takes another mouthful, clearly enjoying this.

"Haven't you both got homework to do?" I snap, completely lacking in anything better to say.

Ronan smirks and nudges Ruby's elbow. "Come on, that's Mum speak for clear off. Let's leave them to their boring chat." Ronan pulls Ruby out of the room by her sweater sleeve leaving us alone again.

"She doesn't know what she's talking about half the time." I laugh, flustered. *Could this be any more embarrassing?*

"It's quite alright, I really should be going now anyway." As he stands, his eyes seem to leisurely take in my appearance from bottom to top making the hairs on the back of my neck stand up. He places his mug on the drainer and picks up the paperwork.

"Well thanks again for dropping by, I appreciate your help with Ronan." I say as I walk behind him to the door to see him out. I feel a bit more composed without his intense eyes on me and a little distance between us. He suddenly stops a few steps short of the door and turns to me causing me to bump into him. Before I can move back, he takes hold of the hand on his chest and holds it there firmly in place as he leans into my ear.

"If I can be of any other assistance Miss Wells, be sure to let me know," he whispers.

The sensation of his breath against my cheek and his physical contact has my head spinning and I'm not thinking straight. I stretch up on to my toes and kiss his cheek, taking both of us by surprise.

"You can call me Amanda," I whisper back.

He raises an eyebrow at me seductively, as if I've just laid down the gauntlet. He nods farewell once and then leaves closing the door behind him. *What the fuck was I thinking? This can't happen in any way shape or form, can it?*

Before panic completely takes over, I take my phone out of pocket and dial my sister.

"You're never going to believe what just happened."

Chapter Four

Tyler

The swarm of students in the corridor parts like the Red Sea as I stride through moments after the bell sounds. It would seem that in the short time I've been here, I have already earned a reputation as someone not to be crossed. I don't mean to give off this vibe, but it's been the same in every school I've worked in. I think sometimes my passion and drive for what I do can come across as stern and harsh.

I had hoped to have more time to prepare for this parent's meeting but unfortunately the day didn't pan out as expected. I usually like to have some rehearsed phrases ready up my sleeve because parents can be ruthless. Especially ones who are worried about their children's education, which is understandable, but difficult to handle nonetheless.

As I arrive at the hall, most of the students have left the premises now and a few of the parents have started to gather at the door for the meeting. It always amazes me how quickly teenagers can evacuate the building when they hear the bell and yet almost move in slow motion when you ask them to do something in class. Pam is hovering at the front of the hall, fussing with piles of newsletters I had her print earlier in the day.

"There you are Mr Woodgate," she says hurriedly. *I don't know why she's looking so flustered, it's not her giving the speech!* "Did you remember to bring your USB stick with the presentation on?"

"Yes, Pam, believe it or not I am a fully functioning adult who gets shit done even when you're not around!" I snap. I instantly feel bad and glance around the empty hall to double check no one else was in earshot.

Pam looks shocked by my unnecessary outburst and tries to busy herself elsewhere.

"I'm very sorry. There was no need to snap at you like that and there was definitely no need to swear. Can I let you in on a secret?"

She looks a little less hurt as intrigue takes over. She nods at me and offers a small smile.

"Even though I've been doing this job for years, speaking in front of groups of parents still scares me. It makes me tetchy." I whisper theatrically, making her laugh. "I feel like I'm about to get fed to the lions."

"What, a big, fully functioning adult such as yourself? Sounds like you need to pull your socks up and get shit done." She jokes, throwing my own words back in my face.

I raise an eyebrow at her, amused. *Touché. I think I'm going to like working with Pam.*

"I'll be over here if you need anything." Pam offers me an encouraging smile and walks away just as the hall starts to fill with parents.

Taking a deep breath, I glance over my notes while the chairs fill and the room becomes loud with chatter. Even over all the noise, I'm instantly aware the moment Amanda arrives. I hear the sound of her high heels on the hardwood floor and I know it's her. I can't look up because if I do, I'll get lost in thoughts of red satin ruffles and stilettos.

To my complete and utter surprise, I get through most of my speech without fault. I'm aware of the sexy red blur in my peripheral vision but make a conscious effort *not* to make eye contact or even look in her general direction. As my speech about my vision for the school and how I plan to achieve it, comes to a close, I open the floor for questions. Amanda's hand shoots straight up. *Fuck.*

"Yes, Miss Wells, isn't it?" I ask as I look directly at her for the first time tonight, trying to make out I'm not completely and utterly aware of *exactly* who she is. I drink her in as I wait for her question. She's back in her uniform today, a mass of red ruffles at her chest and a tight black suit dress. I can't see her shoes but I know at the end of those killer legs will be a pair of patent heels. I can feel the heat rising to my collar as I wait the agonising two seconds it takes for her to ask her question.

"Isn't it true, Mr Woodgate that one of your strategies to improve pupil wellbeing is to put a more stringent behaviour policy in place so that inappropriate behaviour and bullying is less prevalent?"

Before I have a chance to respond, another parent in the row in front of Amanda comments, "Well you would know," under her breath but loudly enough for the room to hear.

Amanda's face turns as scarlet as her uniform. "I beg your pardon?"

The woman in front turns around to face Amanda, "Well you've hardly raised angels have you? I heard just this week that your two almost got suspended. Shame they didn't really."

"Ladies, I think this is a discussion for another time. If you have any concerns regarding the current behaviour policy then I encourage you to come see me in my office after this meeting." I interrupt their exchange and try to put out the fire before it gets going. I should stop there but I can't help myself from adding; "We do not publicly name and shame students here and we do not listen to or spread malicious gossip." I look directly at the woman in front of Amanda and from the look on her face, I think I have made my point clear. She shrinks down in her chair and looks away. I don't look back at Amanda but I can tell from the rise and fall of her chest that she's upset by the outburst.

"If there are no further questions then I would like to thank you all for coming and I hope to see you all as the year goes on. Good night."

I turn my back on the crowd and start to shut down the laptop and projector as everyone starts to leave. When I turn back around, Amanda is gone. I'm not sure if I'm sad or relieved. I'm not sure what I would say to her in such a public place. *How are you supposed to act professional around someone who literally sets your soul on fire?*

As the last of the parents leave the room, I send Pam home for the evening and head back to my office to get the keys to lock up. I told Mike, the caretaker not to worry tonight as I was going to be here. Just as I round the corner to the corridor leading to my office, the door to the ladies swings open and I collide with a puffy-eyed Amanda. She grabs hold of the lapels of my suit jacket to steady herself and some of my papers fall to the floor.

Without a second's thought about what I'm doing, I grab her by the forearms and bundle her through the nearest doorway which happens to lead to the art supplies store, leaving a flurry of paperwork on the floor outside. The door closes, leaving us in pitch black and I push her against it, finding her lips in the darkness. I could see when she came out of the bathroom that she had been crying but now I can taste the salt from her tears as I smudge her freshly applied lipstick. Her urgency, matches my own and she claws at my suit and tie pulling me even closer to her. I can feel every curve of her pressed up against me and I harden against her thigh. A small moan escapes her lips and I swallow it along with one of my own. The only other sound is our ragged breathing as we take what we need from each other. *This is complete and utter madness.*

Some sort of rational thoughts try to fight their way from my subconscious but I ignore them for now, too lost in the sheer pleasure of the moment.

"Please don't cry." I eventually whisper when our lips part for breath. I instead kiss the side of her neck and twirl her curls round my finger.

"Sorry," she whispers back, breathless. "Sometimes they make me so mad. They have no right to judge."

"Don't let them get to you. You're incredible." I murmur, my lips still never leaving her skin as they dance along her jawline back towards her lips.

"Thank you for defending me in there."

That's the moment my sensible subconscious breaks through and starts screaming at me. *What the fuck are you doing?* I'm meant to be a professional. I'm in a position of power and trust and yet here I am, passionately kissing a parent in the art cupboard. I've lost my goddamn mind.

"I have to be careful, Amanda. I can't be seen to have favourites. This..." I gesture in the darkness between the two of us, "Can't happen."

She stands perfectly still for a second and I brace myself for her reaction as I can't see her facial expression.

"And yet it is" she whispers seductively as she slides her hand over my hard length and grips me through my trousers. *Holy fuck.* I moan against her neck and fist my hand in her hair.

"Why do I get the feeling you're going to be a one-way ticket to the end of my career?"

"I don't know...Sir." She whispers it so quietly I'm not entirely certain I heard her right.

"What did you just call me?" I ask, taking her chin in my hand and tilting her lips towards mine.

"Sir," she repeats.

Never has my cock responded to a word as instantaneously as it is right now. I push Amanda back against the door and slide my knee between her legs forcing them to part. She rubs against my leg as I rush to untie her red neckerchief and let it fall to the floor. She leans up and kisses me again as I rip open the buttons on her blouse, sending them scattering to the floor in the darkness. I just start to unbutton my trousers when my work phone lights up and starts ringing in my pocket.

"Shit," I curse as I try to get my breathing under control to answer the phone. I take the phone from my pocket and in the little bit of light it provides I can see Amanda's lipstick is smudged and her lips are swollen from the intensity of our kiss. Her hair is wild and I can see her deep cleavage that I exposed only seconds go rising and falling as she too tries to regain some control.

"Mr Woodgate speaking." I manage to say with some sort or normality. As soon as I answer the call, I know I have to deal with this urgently and the moment is over. I finish the call and hang up but let the light on my phone remain, so I can see Amanda's face.

"I'm so sorry, duty calls." I tell her. "I won't be long. Stay here and I'll come back and walk you out once everyone has definitely left the building."

As soon as the words leave my mouth, I regret how they sound, as if she's some dirty little secret. I kiss her on the cheek and leave, closing the door behind me. In the harsh light of the corridor, I pick up my paperwork before making my way to my office. The enormity and potential repercussions of what I've just done weighing heavy on my chest.

I conclude my business as quickly as I can but when I return to the storeroom, Amanda has gone. I pull the light cord and see her red neckerchief lying on the floor along with a handful of buttons. I pick them up and stuff them into my pocket. *Shit. What have I done?*

Chapter Five

Amanda

"Muuuuum? Have you seen my skinny jeans?" Ruby hollers from somewhere upstairs. *Why can't these kids use their legs to walk to me when they want to talk to me? Why do they have to shout through the house?*

"Muuuuum!" she shouts again before I've even had a chance to put down the cup of tea I optimistically made myself. I haven't started and finished a hot one in years. I sigh and stomp up the stairs to Ruby's room to find her straightening her hair in the mirror.

"Where are my jeans?" she snaps, the moment I step into the room.

"You mean the ones sat right there on the top of your ironing pile that I did a week ago?" I lean against the doorframe and fold my arms.

"Oh, yeah, "she mumbles and turns her attention back to her hair.

"You're welcome," I roll my eyes as I leave her to it. I stick my head into Ronan's room as I walk past. "You ok, bud?"

A sound resembling a grunt comes from the other side of the room but he doesn't look up. He's too engrossed in whatever vile computer game he's currently playing so I take the opportunity to go back to my cup of tea.

Sitting on the sofa, I absentmindedly pick at the two-week-old nail varnish that desperately needs redoing. Maybe I'll have time later. Ruby is going for a sleepover at her friend's house soon and Ronan barely leaves his room. I start to feel excited by the prospect of an evening to myself to paint my nails in my pyjamas. I could even get myself a bottle of wine. I almost laugh out loud at how tragic it is that this is what excites me now. This is considered a good evening.

Still, things have not exactly been uneventful of late. Images of my encounter with Mr Woodgate the other night flash through my mind like some sort of erotic slideshow. We only really kissed essentially but it felt so much naughtier than that. Heat floods my cheeks at the memory of it, I'm not entirely sure if it's from lust or embarrassment or quite probably both. *What on earth was I thinking?* I have never done anything like that before. Ever! I still can't get over how bold I suddenly was, I can only put it down to the darkness and the adrenaline giving me false confidence.

Not that it did me much good. That was four days ago and I haven't seen or heard from him since. He's probably realised what a terrible idea getting involved with a parent would be and has gone cold. Can't say that I blame him, it really would be a terrible decision on his part. It was nice while it lasted - all ten minutes of it.

Once Ruby leaves, I knock and let Ronan know that I'm popping out to collect a few supplies. He nods and mumbles something incoherent as he blasts alien blood and guts across the TV screen. *Nice.* It's cold outside so I grab my oversized grey cardigan on the way out. It's hideously baggy and stretched but it's so cosy. It might be even older than my children, many of my clothes are. I'm certain I've got underwear lurking in my bottom drawer that predates the twins. *How depressing.*

The local supermarket is only a few streets away so I'm there in no time at all. By the time my arms are full with a bottle of wine, a tub of ice cream, a new nail colour and some trashy magazines, I'm regretting not getting a basket. I pack all my non-essentials into a carrier bag and brave the cold again. It got dark in the time it took me to choose between chocolate chip and strawberry.

I scurry along the dimly lit street, clutching my assortment of shopping, desperately wishing I'd worn more than just a cardigan. The temperature has really dropped now and it doesn't help that I'm hugging a bag with a tub of ice cream in it.

To my absolute horror, I spot Mr Woodgate, *Tyler*, on the opposite side of the street walking this way, talking to another member of staff. Mrs Bray, maybe? I'm not sure of her name but I'm pretty sure she used to teach Ronan for Maths.

Shit. I must look like I belong in an outtake of Bridget Jones' Diary for God sake. *Could I be any more tragic?* I haven't seen or spoken to him since our encounter in the cupboard and I have no idea what the appropriate thing is to say in this situation. *Hey, nice to see you again, did you manage to find any of my shirt buttons? Or, did you know when I lay awake at night I still think about your hands on me?* Gah!

Maybe I can just keep walking and pretend I didn't see them? *Yes, I'll do that.* I speed up a bit and keep my eyes firmly trained on the pavement in front of me, praying I don't fall flat on my face and make a complete tit out of myself.

"Miss Wells?" Mrs Bray's loud and imposing voice hits me from across the street. *Wonderful.*

I look up and smile awkwardly at them both as they cross the street towards me. Mr Woodgate looks as uncomfortable as I feel but is clearly trying to hide it.

Mrs Bray is all smiles as she approaches me. "I thought that was you! I couldn't stop without saying hello and finding out how Ronan is getting on."

I smile politely and focus all of my attention on her, afraid to make eye contact with Mr Woodgate for fear of melting into a puddle along with my ice cream, right here in the street.

"He has his ups and downs but his grades are good." I try to keep my answer short and sweet in the hopes that she'll let me go and I can escape this uncomfortable nightmare. "Anyway, I best run, my ice cream's going to melt."

"And what about Ruby? How is she getting on this year? Such a promising young lady." Mrs Bray ignores my attempts to shut the conversation down and carries on, oblivious.

I muster another polite smile and take a deep breath. Chancing a quick glance at Mr Woodgate or Tyler, whatever he wants me to call him, I instantly wish I hadn't. His eyes shine with amusement as he tries to stifle a grin.

"Ruby is very well, thank you. I really must be going now."

Mrs Bray gives me a wave goodbye and I hurry down the road as fast as I can to put as much distance as possible between us. *Awkward as fuck.* Foolishly I start to overthink the brief encounter. *How embarrassing. What must he think of me?* I could literally crawl into a hole and die right now. Hopefully if my children keep out of trouble I'll be able to stay out of his way and not see him again.

I turn down the side street that leads to my house as I contemplate the extremely slim chance of that actually happening. Ronan can't stay out of trouble. Conflict finds him wherever he goes.

"Amanda," a breathless sounding voice comes from behind me, along with the sound of hurried footsteps.

I turn to see Mr Woodgate catch up to me with a jog.

"Have you got a minute?"

I smile, despite the awkward weirdness between us.

"Sorry about just now. That's hardly how I hoped to see you again. I wanted to know if you were alright after the other evening." He looks at me with concern and regret. "That was unacceptable of me. I can only apologise."

"It wasn't just you that was involved, as I remember it." I reply coyly.

His eyes blaze with something altogether different, a sudden surge of passion igniting in them. He takes a step closer to me and I can feel his warmth cutting through the cold night air.

"It was an error in judgement," he murmurs.

"I'm sorry you feel that way."

He's so close to me now, both of us watching the other with a matched intensity. His lips part ever so slightly as he takes in my face, edging subtly closer and closer. Our warm breath mingles and visibly entwines between us in the cold sliver of night air that separates us.

I close my eyes, ready to feel his lips meet mine when the air suddenly stirs and he steps back.

"I meant what I said Amanda. This can't happen again. I'm so sorry."

Dumbstruck and feeling like an idiot, I open my eyes and watch as he jogs back round the corner from where he came without so much as a backward glance. I wrap my cardigan tighter around myself and hurry home. My sad little bag of trashy magazines and ice cream has never been more fitting. *You're an idiot, Amanda. They're all the same.*

Chapter Six

Tyler

Subtly I check my wristwatch, trying not to make it obvious how much I want this staff meeting to be over. It's been running for over an hour already and it's still going. Mr Campbell has been discussing the finer details of the reasons why we shouldn't stock carbonated drinks in the canteen and I'm about to lose my mind or die of boredom, whichever comes first. I look around the staffroom to see more than a few faces looking as uninterested as I feel so I swiftly try to wrap up Mr Campbell's ramblings so we can move on and go home.

"Any other business?" I finally get to ask the sea of bored faces.

It's no shock that this school's standards are failing, the staff are quite possibly the most uninspiring bunch of people I've ever met. The students must lose the will to live on a daily basis. *Things need to change around here, and fast.*

The Head of the Art department raises her hand as I pause for a sip of my coffee, waiting to see if anyone has anything to say. I nod at Miss Lamb, encouraging her to go on.

"I'd just like to remind everyone about keeping the art store tidy," she waves her hands around in the air theatrically, causing all the bangles up her arms to jangle.

Resisting the urge to roll my eyes, I sip more of my coffee instead. *Really? We're going to spend our Friday evening discussing the state of the art cupboard?*

"Just the other day I found several buttons spilled all over the floor in there!" She exclaims dramatically.

I choke on my coffee, trying not to spray it everywhere as I realise she's referring to Amanda's blouse buttons. A few of the staff stop to look at my outburst as I try to compose myself and mop up the coffee down my shirt. Visions of me slamming Amanda against the door and tearing open her blouse fill my mind as I desperately try to squash them down.

"I'm fine, please carry on." I choke.

"As I was saying, it's important that we take care of the limited resources we have and not be careless or reckless."

Careless and reckless is about right.

"Thank you for that reminder." I smile, with as much professionalism as I can muster. "If there isn't anything else then please have a lovely weekend everyone."

I breathe a sigh of relief as the staff pack up their stuff and leave. It's been another long week and I can't wait to get out of here. Maybe I should call Tom and see if he's free this weekend to come to the Lake House with me. It'd do me good to get some distance and perspective. My younger brother of two years is always up for a getaway.

When I get back to my office, I rummage around in my briefcase for my phone. My hand finds the silky smoothness of Amanda's neckerchief stuffed in the bottom corner and I pull it out, running the material between my finger and thumb. The memory instantly makes me hard as I lift it to my face and inhale the scent of her perfume. *What are you doing?* My fascination and lack of self control around this woman is dangerous, bordering on obsession.

I drop the red fabric back into my briefcase as if it burned me, desperately trying to shake off the spell Amanda unknowingly has over me. Hastily I find my phone and dial Tom's number. He answers after the first ring.

"Big brother," he greets. "What's up?"

"Everything," I mutter, looking down at the raging hard on I'm trying to suppress.

"Oh dear, that doesn't sound good. Care to share?"

"I've got myself into a bit of bother. Are you up for the Lake House?" I ask as I shove all my stuff into my briefcase and lock my office door.

"You bet. I'll pick you up in an hour."

• • • ● • ● • ● • •

True to his word, Tom arrives outside my house one hour later and beeps the horn. He drives a great big four-wheel drive that looks like it's designed for scaling mountains even though he only drives to work and back these days. Tom works as a photographer, a very good one at that and owns his own studio on the other side of town.

He smiles and waves as I approach his monster truck and throw my bag in the back.

"Is this a bottled beer kind of weekend or a stiff whiskey kind of weekend?" He chuckles as I get in the passenger seat beside him.

"Definitely stiff whiskey."

Tom raises his eyebrows and whistles as he pulls out into the evening traffic. Thankfully it doesn't take long to get there and before we know it we are sitting on the wraparound porch of our family lake house watching the water ripple in the dark. Our parents bought this place when they retired but they rarely came here once their health declined.

"Lay it on me, brother. What's weighing you down? I'm going to guess it's either a woman or work."

I lean back in my seat and puff out my cheeks, looking out at the dark lake. "Both actually. A woman at work."

Tom starts grinning like an idiot. "No way. My squeaky clean big brother with the untarnished halo is banging a member of his own staff? Ha!"

Tom slaps his hand on his thigh and laughs as he swings his beer, looking like the cat that got the cream.

"It's worse than that. She's a parent." I cringe, feeling even worse now that I've said it out loud.

Tom's jaw drops as he turns to face me.

"I haven't had sex with her," I add hastily.

"But you want to?"

"More than I can stand," I admit. "It's a nightmare, Tom. She's all I think about. It's like I become someone else when she's around and I can't help myself. I know the consequences if we get caught in school but as soon as she's near me, I lose all sense of reason." I realise I've been rambling and shut myself up with a large mouthful of whiskey.

"Sheesh, sounds like you've got it bad. How does she feel about it all?"

"It's hard to say, I bundled her into a store cupboard and kissed the life out of her, ripping her shirt open in the process. Then I got called away and avoided her ever since, except I bumped into her in the street and almost kissed her again. What am I going to do, Tom?"

Tom blinks, looking at me in surprise. "Maybe start with not assaulting her in cupboards?" he jokes. "You might want to slow things down to a normal speed."

"There is no normal! This is not normal. This is so unprofessional and cannot happen in any way." I butt in.

"Buuuut?" Tom smirks.

"I can't stand the thought of that being it between us." I slump down in my chair feeling defeated. "If I give in to this, my career could be over."

"Only if you get caught," he chirps.

I roll my eyes and mutter. "That always was your motto."

Tom grins and stands up, stretching his arms out. "It's served me well. I say live a little, brother. You've always played by the rules and put work first. Maybe it's time you thought about what you really want." Tom disappears inside with his empty beer bottle, probably in search of another.

I sit quietly pondering his words, looking out at the inky black expanse in front of me. I've always been the one enforcing the rules, not the one breaking them. I always thought it would be an impossible habit to break until those long legs of Amanda's crossed themselves in front of my desk and bewitched me. *I really am royally fucked.*

Tom's voice calls from somewhere inside. "Come on, stop moping so I can kick your arse at a game of pool."

Chapter Seven

Amanda

It might only be September but the wind is bitterly cold as it blows across the football field. *What a way to spend my Sunday mornings.* I cling to my polystyrene cup filled with what I'm told is coffee. I won't actually drink it, it's the ghastly instant stuff that tastes like a puddle but it is keeping my hands warm at least.

This has been my Sunday morning ritual for years now, watching Ronan at football practice, freezing my tits off while Ruby whines and complains about the cold, the rain, the boredom, the hunger, well everything mostly. I can think of better ways to spend my weekends but I do it for Ronan. He enjoys it and he lets off some much needed steam. These are the sacrifices you make as a parent. It's not like his dad has ever shown up for practice or even a game. In fact, he hasn't shown up for anything since the day I left with the kids.

"Mum, how much longer is it?" Ruby huffs, briefly looking up from her book.

"Another ten minutes, love. It's almost finished."

Ruby is sitting on the bench next to me with her knees drawn up and her coat hood pulled up over her head so you can barely see her face through all the fur. I don't need to see her face to know that her eyes are rolling though.

"Can I at least get hot chocolate at the end?"

"Yes, yes," I mutter dismissively, totally preoccupied by the fight that's about to break out between Ronan and another player. *Shit.*

"That's if your brother doesn't get knocked out beforehand," I add.

I watch in exasperation as Ronan squares up to the other boy and shoves him hard in the chest, causing him to stumble backwards but he doesn't fall. The referee blows his whistle desperately hard as he jogs over to them both. Ronan takes no notice and advances on the boy again who takes a swing at him but misses.

"Ronan!" I shout across the pitch but my efforts are futile.

Ronan sees and hears only what he wants to when he gets like this. It's as if the red mist descends and shuts off all his senses. An unfortunate trait he inherited from his father.

The referee blows his whistle again and shouts at them to separate but by now they're rolling in the mud, swinging at each other like a pair of crazed apes. *Give me strength.*

"Ronan!" I holler again before taking off at a sprint across the pitch.

I know I'm not meant to interfere but I can't watch as they beat each other black and blue.

"So embarrassing," I hear Ruby mutter as she sinks further into her coat.

I reach Ronan just as the referee is attempting to pull the other boy off of him. He was slightly bigger than Ronan and managed to gain the upper hand.

"Ronan! What are you doing?" I scold at the same time as offering him my hand to help him up out of the mud.

"Just leave it, Mum! I'm fine!" He growls as he gets himself up off the floor, ignoring my hand. Ronan walks away with me in tow but not before he's shouted across the pitch as the boy walks in the opposite direction. "If he wasn't such a prick, it wouldn't have started!"

"Ronan!" I hiss under my breath, completely embarrassed at all the eyes on me and my son right now.

Had I realised how often I was going to say his name in vain, I would've called him something else. I love the name Ronan and yet it has become a daily curse word in our house.

"Are you hurt?" I ask him when we get back to where Ruby is still huddled in her coat.

"I'm fine," he snaps.

I can already see the beginnings of a black eye and there's blood smeared along his forearm that he's wiped from heaven knows where.

I sigh in exasperation.

"Can we have hot chocolate now?" Ruby pipes up from beneath her hood, completely unphased by the sight of her bloodied and bruised brother.

I squeeze my eyes shut and rub at my temples. "Just take my purse and go and get what you want." I have no energy left to argue.

Turning back to Ronan, I open my mouth to lecture him on all the reasons why his behaviour is not acceptable when the other boy's Dad comes marching over. *This is all I need.*

"You should keep that kid of yours on a tighter leash!" He spits out angrily as he approaches. *Geez, hostile much?*

"Excuse me?" I reply, folding my arms across my chest. We both know I heard him perfectly well.

"Your kid, he's a menace. What sort of mother lets their son carry on like that? Look at my boy!" The angry man is tomato red and gesticulating at his sullen looking son across the other side of the field.

"Don't speak to my mum like that!" Ronan's temper rears its ugly head once again. "It's nothing to do with her. I punched your son because he's a cheating scumbag."

The man looks positively shocked at Ronan's brazen honesty and lack of remorse. He's a lot of things my son, but he's no liar.

"Calm down, Ronan. Go and help your sister." I say in an attempt to diffuse the situation. Ronan says nothing more but he doesn't move either. He continues to glare at the kid's dad.

"Listen, I'm sorry you're so angry but from what I saw, your son gave as good as he got and he almost certainly threw the first punch."

"And that makes it alright does it?" The man scoffs. "With a parenting attitude like that, it's no wonder he's the way he is."

OK, now I'm pissed.

"I'm sorry, and where were you exactly when their fight broke out?" I reply sarcastically, putting my hands on my hips to prevent me from using them for anything else. *So, maybe Ronan isn't just like his dad.*

"Maybe if you'd been paying attention instead of drinking lager in the clubhouse before midday then you would have seen your little shit hit my son first. Climb down off your high horse and go and ruin someone else's day."

The man just stands there gaping at me like a fish. I don't give him a chance to respond, I turn around and march across the field away from him towards the car.

"Ronan, let's go." I call over my shoulder.

He catches up to me in a few paces. "How did you know he was drinking at the bar?"

"Lucky guess."

"You know you're pretty badass sometimes." Ronan mumbles.

"Just get in the car, I need a cup of tea."

Ruby joins us with her cup of steaming hot chocolate and slides into the back clicking her seat belt on just in time for me to start revving out of the car park.

It's been a long day and it's not even lunchtime.

• • • ● • ● • ● • • •

The twins are downstairs watching a movie now that we've finished dinner. I was completely shocked that it only took them ten minutes to agree on one, so I thought I'd take the opportunity to run myself a hot bath and soak the stress of the day away.

I lie in the hot bubbly water sipping a glass of wine and absentmindedly scroll through my phone. I don't know why I bother, it's all complete nonsense but it gets me out of my own head for a while. If I'm thinking about what Sally down the road had for dinner on her latest diet regime then I'm not thinking about my own shit storm of a life.

It doesn't take long though for my thoughts to wander to Tyler Woodgate. *I wonder if he's on social media?* I doubt it, being in his position but I can't help myself but look him up anyway. I find nothing, just as I thought. A quick tap into a search engine however does bring up a heart-stoppingly handsome photo of him taken by the local newspaper about five years ago. The article describes him as the 'Hot-Shot Head from Highview'. The brief news story outlines how he captured the attention of the community by bringing Highview Secondary out of its failing status and producing outstanding results.

I sigh and place my phone down on the edge of the bath, replacing it with my wine glass. *It must be nice to achieve something. Like, really be successful at something.* All I've ever managed to achieve was not getting fired, well mostly. There was that one time when I threw up all over a customer back when I worked in the newsagents in my teens. I was so hungover that one whiff of their bacon sandwich had me hurling my guts all over them. I'm pretty sure I got fired from that job, I didn't stick around long enough to find out.

Sipping on my wine, I stare at the snake tattoo that winds around my upper thigh, mocking me from beneath the bubbles. *Stupid thing*. I had it done when I was eighteen and thought I really was a badass as Ronan put it. *I wasn't*. I cried like a baby the whole way through, it stung like a bitch and I have regretted it ever since.

I think about the twins and all the ways they have yet to fuck up their lives. Parenting is a crazy, fine line between wanting to wrap them up and protect them from the world and all its bullshit and also wanting them to be fierce enough to take it on. If only they knew that most of us spend the best part of the day just winging it and hoping for the best.

I drain my glass and decide to get out of the bath and do something productive like make the packed lunches or solve world famine, but as I step out I manage to knock my phone off the edge and down into the water.

Shit. One step at a time, Amanda. No world domination for you tonight.

Chapter Eight

Tyler

Parent's evening. The date in every teacher's diary that fills their heart with dread. Knowing that they will have to give up their evening to listen to countless parents air their petty grievances and deny all knowledge that their child can be the devil himself when their back is turned.

Luckily for me, I'm not here to meet with parents, just to be present and offer a helping hand if needed. Of course, there is one parent I'm hoping to see tonight, even if only from a distance. The pathetic level to which I've stooped is truly astounding. I smirk at myself and shake my head, thrusting my hands in my trouser pockets as I pace the large hall keeping an eye on things.

I hear her before I see her. The tell-tale click of her high heels across the wooden floor instantly stirs something below my belt that needs to be quashed immediately, so I try not to look for her. Instead I go to the water dispenser, turning my back on the room to pour myself a cup of cold water. I take my time sipping the ice cold liquid, delaying turning around. *I'm acting like one of my students. This is ridiculous.*

I take a deep breath and turn, looking out across the room. It takes me a second or two to spot her but she's there. I find Amanda sitting across the table with Ronan and Ruby either side of her, already deep in conversation with Ruby's English teacher. Her elegant legs are crossed under the table. I can't see what colour her heels are today but she's in her work uniform. *Does she ever get a day off? She works more hours than me!*

Amanda smiles at Mrs Panchet and the sound of her laugh carries across the room and grips me by the balls. She tucks a few loose strands of her hair behind her ear as she speaks and wets her bottom lip with her tongue. I realise then that I've been staring and quickly clear my throat, walking away in the opposite direction.

"Mr Woodgate," a member of the PE department calls my name and I'm thankful for the distraction. "Would you mind speaking to Mr and Mrs Goodman about their issues regarding the PE uniform please? It seems my opinion counts for zilch," he mutters under his breath.

"Of course," I chuckle. "Lead the way."

Mr and Mrs Goodman are notoriously difficult. I've only been here a matter of weeks and I already know them well. Their Year 8 daughter is somewhat of a pampered princess who is unfamiliar with the word 'no'. *This should be fun.*

Twenty minutes later and I'm still listening to all the reasons why girls should not be made to wear a polo shirt and shorts for physical activities. *Who knew there were so many?!* The urge to roll my eyes is overwhelming but I somehow manage to maintain a polite and professional persona, even when I'm told how my 'archaic ways are crushing their daughter's inner goddess.' *Is this shit for real?* I'm half expecting a hidden film crew to jump out at any moment and tell me it's all a prank. Unfortunately for me, they're deadly serious.

To add to my nightmare, Amanda's shoes click their way across the floor towards me as she slides into the seat opposite the teacher nearest me. The air stirs with her perfume and my cock twitches at the sound of her voice. I daren't look at her, it'll be game over. Instead I continue to feign interest in what Mr and Mrs Goodman have to say as I readjust my tie. *It's gotten awfully hot in here all of a sudden.*

Amanda listens to what Ronan's Humanities teacher has to say but her eyes wander my way more than once. I can feel them on me. I clear my throat and once again try to wrap up my conversation. *I need some air.*

"Thank you so much for your suggestions. I'll be sure to raise them with the board of Governers," I tell the huffy parents, who are already busy looking up on their phones who they should escalate their complaint to.

I take the opportunity to slip out and escape to my office. *This is fucking insanity. How can one woman get so far under my skin?* I need to get it together. I have a job to do, an important one and yet my thoughts are dominated by Amanda and her killer legs almost constantly.

I undo my tie and let it hang down my chest, making the decision there and then that I won't go back out there. I've shown my face, that's all that's required. There are plenty of other members of the Senior Leadership Team should there be any problems. My time would be better spent at home, working through the data reports.

I gather up my stuff into my briefcase and am just about to leave for the night when there's a gentle knock at the door. *Now what?*

"Come in," I bark, a little gruffer than I meant to.

I look up to see Amanda slide in through my door, only opening it a small amount. Her heels are in her hand, which would explain why I didn't hear her coming. I notice her delicate bare feet on the mahogany floor. Her toenails are the same brilliant shade of red as her shoes and neck scarf.

"Amanda," I say with surprise as she closes the door behind her and looks at me almost shyly. "What are you doing up here?"

"I'm not entirely sure." She looks down at her hands holding her shoes in front of her.

"Where are Ruby and Ronan?" I walk as casually over to her as I can manage. I feel anything but casual. I feel as if I might burst into flames and burn from the inside out.

"Gone to get snacks from the tuck shop."

"I see," I take one hand out of my trouser pocket and rub it across my trimmed beard, contemplating the situation I now find myself in.

"So, you have approximately ten minutes to spare?" I ask slowly, as I reach her.

"Yes," she whispers, looking up at me. Her back now pressed against my heavy wooden door.

"And you thought you'd spend those minutes up here, with me?" I raise an eyebrow.

"Yes," she breathes.

I watch her as she watches me. Neither of us moves or speaks. The only sound is that of our laboured breathing as the air thickens with tension and unspoken desires. Before I can overthink this and talk myself out of it, I reach across and turn the key in the lock, causing a loud, formidable click. It's the sound of secrets and seduction. A promise of what's to come.

Scooping Amanda up under her arms I lift and carry her the short distance to my desk. She wraps her arms around my neck, causing her heels which are still in her hands to dig into my back. I sit her down hurriedly on the edge and the material of her tight skirt strains against her thighs as they part for me. Groaning at the sight of her, I knot my fingers in her wavy hair and pull her towards me as I hungrily devour her lips. She tastes like mint gum and smells like her usual perfume. The scent has been firmly imprinted in my brain since the first time I laid eyes on her.

Amanda grips the loose tie that hangs round my shoulders and uses it to pull me even closer. Every inch of her is wrapped around me as if we had been fused into one being. I feel like a horny teenage boy, I can't get enough. Despite every inch of her curves being pressed tightly against me, it's still not enough. She's not close enough, I crave so much more. It's a desperate need that I've never felt before, like I'm gasping for air and Amanda is oxygen.

"This is insanity," I murmur against her lips as I pull back just enough for my hands to be able to roam down the front of her blouse.

"Then I'll willingly lose my mind," she whispers back, gently sucking on my neck, just above my collar.

Amanda reaches for her buttons and is about to start undoing them but I cover her hand with mine, stopping her. I'd love nothing more than to rip it open once again but I stop myself and her.

"Not like this. You deserve so much more than this. I need to see you, properly." I pant, wrestling with myself over putting a stop to things. "Let me get to know you."

Amanda smiles as she catches her breath. "Like a date?"

"Sort of, except not a public one," I clarify. "Come with me to my family's lake house. I want to treat you right, make you feel special."

I pepper a row of kisses along her jaw, starting at her ear and ending at the corner of her mouth. Amanda sighs happily and tightens her grip around my neck.

"Hurried fumbles in cupboards and offices isn't good enough. You deserve better." I utter against her neck as my lips continue their trail down to her collarbone.

"I quite enjoy them," she whispers darkly, closing her eyes and tipping her head back to expose more skin for me to kiss. "But I admire the sentiment, Sir."

A low rumble erupts deep in my throat before I can stop it.

"Amanda," I warn, pushing her backwards so she's laid flat on my desk with her legs wrapped around my waist still. "You're making it really hard to do the right thing."

"Then don't." Amanda looks at me with more hunger than I've ever experienced before and it's enough to make me crack.

I grip her thighs with desperate fingers and watch as her skirt rides up high enough to expose her lacy black underwear. It's then I notice the snake tattoo wrapped seductively around the top of her leg and the sight only spurs me on more. *She really is full of surprises.*

I climb up and over her on the desk, delivering the final blow to my moral compass, smashing it into oblivion.

Amanda's soft curves press against me as I lay on top of her and crash my lips to hers. My hard length strains against my zipper between her open legs and she writhes against it creating an almost unbearable friction. I've never craved anything like I crave her. Addiction has never been a problem for me, until now.

Hurriedly, I untuck her blouse from her skirt so I can run my fingers over her bare stomach. My hand travels higher up inside her blouse until I find the lace edge of her bra and my hand moulds itself around her full tits. Amanda moans softly into my mouth and pushes against my hand. I grip her harder in response, digging my fingers in and kneading her firmly. I feel her nipple harden against my palm making the urge to be inside her overwhelming.

I'm about to cross a line I can't come back from when Amanda's phone rings loudly on the desk beside us. Ruby's name flashes on the screen as the device vibrates loudly across the wood dragging us back to reality and chasing away the lust fuelled fog that had enveloped us both.

I stand up and back away from Amanda as if she were a live wire about to electrocute me. Amanda readjusts her hair and clothing hurriedly while she tries to control her breathing.

"Hi," she answers, trying not to sound out of breath. "I'm just coming."

Amanda looks at me guiltily from beneath her dark lashes. "Wait for me by the car."

Amanda slides the phone into her handbag and steps off the desk, slipping her feet into her heels without so much as a single word. She doesn't look at me, I think my reaction hurt her feelings.

She turns towards the door but I stop her, gently grabbing her by the forearm and spinning her round.

"I meant what I said. Let me do things right. Let me know when you're free and I'll arrange for us to be at the Lake House."

I sweep some stray strands of hair off of her shoulder and rub the pad of my thumb across her jaw. "I don't ever want to make you feel like my dirty little secret, Amanda."

"You just did." Amanda gives me a sad smile before unlocking the door and disappearing out into the corridor. The fading sound of her heels as she walks away leaves me feeling empty and hollow. *I have no idea what I'm doing.*

Chapter Nine

Amanda

Trolley rage is definitely *a thing* and I am most definitely a sufferer. People in supermarkets are idiots. Like the lady in front of me now, for instance. Her trolley has been abandoned diagonally across the aisle, while she chats to her friend several feet away about brands of laundry detergent. *Why? Why can't you move out of the way and let me go about my business?!*

I try standing politely for a few seconds in the hopes that she'll notice me, but nope. So then I huff and puff a little bit with my hands on my hips but she's still completely oblivious to the fact they are not the only two people in the supermarket right now. In the end I lose patience and nudge her trolley out of the way with mine, a little harder than I meant to and it bumps into a row of jam jars making them wobble precariously. Squeezing past the trolley, I march by as the two women give me the side-eye but don't bother to stop their conversation.

There's just something about doing the weekly food shop that raises my blood pressure and ruins my mood so my next stop is the wine aisle. Whilst I debate the important decision whether to buy one bottle or two, my phone starts to ring in my handbag. It takes a while to find it buried amongst all the junk in there. I come across three hair bands, a half eaten cereal bar of Ruby's, a pair of Ronan's football socks and two dead batteries before eventually finding my phone. *Unknown caller.* Which means it's probably a random sales call.

"Hello?" I huff, not in the mood to be sold double glazing right now.

I tuck the phone under my ear against my shoulder and decide to buy two bottles, grabbing them off the shelf.

"Hi Mandy." The gruff voice on the other end of the phone almost makes me drop the bottles. It's a voice I haven't heard in a very long time but one I recognise instantly.

"Danny?" I squeak in surprise.

The sound of my ex-husband's raspy chuckle makes my skin break out in sweaty goosebumps. *And not the good kind.* The kind where your skin feels like it's crawling and no amount of scrubbing can shake off the discomfort.

"It's been a long time, sugar."

Hearing his old pet name for me makes me feel physically sick and I abandon the idea of finishing the shopping, heading straight for the checkout instead.

"What do you want, Danny?" I spit the words down the phone.

"Can't a man want to talk to his wife without good reason?" His tone is sly and loaded with unspoken bullshit, just like it always was.

"EX-wife," I correct angrily. "And no, you can't actually, not after ten years of radio silence. What is this about?"

I slam the items down on the conveyor belt hurriedly, my hands shaking ever so slightly.

"I want to see my kids."

It's as if time stands still for a moment as I let those dreaded words sink in. They're words I've feared hearing all these years. Until now, he's left us to it, never bothering with the twins. It's sad, but it's better that way. The man is a menace. He doesn't deserve to breathe the same air they do.

"You know that's not going to happen." I hiss, trying not to cause a scene in the supermarket.

"Says who?" he barks. *I knew he couldn't keep his temper for long.*

"Says the piece of paper from the court, Danny!"

The cashier raises her eyebrows but doesn't say a word as she silently scans my items, pretending not to listen to my half of the conversation.

"That's fucking bullshit and you know it. They're my damn kids. You can't keep them from me."

"Watch me." I kill the call, angrily throwing the phone into my bag. I start stuffing groceries into bags like a woman possessed.

The cashier still says nothing but is judging me six ways till Sunday with her eyes. I hear the phone start vibrating again in my bag as she rings up the final items.

"That'll be ninety pounds twenty five," she remarks, eyeing my handbag. She's waiting to see if I'll answer it but it's not happening. That particular conversation is well and truly over.

I pay for my shopping and march out of the supermarket, still accompanied by the sound of my phone vibrating in the depths of my bag. By the time I get home and unpack, I have thirteen missed calls and a fuse so short that I'm ready to go off like an atomic bomb.

The phone lights up and starts buzzing across the countertop once again, daring me to answer it. It's flashing screen taunting me, waiting for me to snap.

I cave in and grab the phone. "Listen, you low life piece of shit. I have nothing more to say to you. Carry on and you can add harassment to your list of misdemeanours."

"Amanda, is everything alright?" An entirely different voice sounds in my ear to the one I was expecting.

"Mr Woodgate!" I squeak in surprise. Embarrassment at the way I just spoke to him floods my cheeks, increasing the temperature in the room by several degrees.

"Just Tyler," he corrects. "Are you alright?"

Something about his authoritative, soothing voice instantly calms me, chasing all the anger away.

"Yes, I'm fine. Sorry about that. I thought you were...someone else."

"Is someone bothering you?" The protective concern in his voice has my ovaries quivering.

"No, everything's fine," I lie. "What can I do for you?"

I try to sound light and breezy to brush him off even though I feel anything but. The knowledge that Danny is back sniffing around has me on high alert.

"Are you home? I want to apologise, in person."

"For what?" Somewhere buried in my subconscious I'm sure there's a niggling reason why I'm supposed to be annoyed with him but with his voice oozing through the phone like melted caramel, I can't for the life of me remember why.

"My behaviour the other night."

"I thought it was me that behaved badly as I remember it." I tease.

A deep, low groan rumbles through the phone, the kind that makes my stomach flutter.

"So, can I come?" I don't miss the double meaning of his words or the way his voice drops an octave.

"Be my guest."

I hang up the phone and sprint up the stairs to the shower. All thoughts of Danny long gone at the prospect of seeing Tyler again. For the next twenty minutes I scrub, shave, primp and pluck until I'm semi-satisfied with what I see in the mirror.

I blow dry my hair and apply my usual red lipstick, matching it with a red off-the-shoulder sweatshirt and black leggings. I want to look nice but not like I'm trying *too* hard. The sound of the doorbell has me giddy as a schoolgirl. *How embarrassing.* I bet that's exactly the reaction he gets on a daily basis as he patrols the corridors in his sharp suit.

"Hi," I smile, breathing in the scent of his aftershave as I open the door.

"Hi," he mirrors back. Except Tyler isn't smiling. He looks positively sinful standing in the shadows of my doorstep with a look in his eyes that can only be described as ravenous. Eyes that unashamedly rake over my body in a way that makes my skin hum.

"Do you want to come in?" I ask, basking in the intensity of his state.

Tyler wets his bottom lip with his tongue making it shine in the dim light.

"No, not with the twins home. I don't trust myself at all," he whispers darkly. "I just needed to see you and apologise."

"Ruby and Ronan aren't here." I inform him with a seductive smirk, opening the door wide in silent invitation.

In a heartbeat, Tyler is through the door kicking it shut behind him and everything instantly becomes a blurry tangle of limbs. His mouth is on mine and his hands are in my hair as he presses me up against the hall wall. Urgency pours from him as he invades all my senses at once. The burn of his short beard across my face as he kisses me in contrast to the softness of his lips is a sensual cocktail. One that I'm becoming intoxicated by at an alarming rate.

"What happened to doing things right?" I pant.

"I'm good at making the rules, not sticking to them. You drive me fucking crazy, Amanda."

He sheds his black overcoat and it falls to the floor with a heavy thud. We take the opportunity of the pause to catch our breath as we stare at one another. We both know what's about to happen and the inevitability of it is tantalising.

"Do you want a cup of coffee?" I taunt, knowing the answer.

"Nope." He steps closer to me like a hunter stalking its prey.

"Glass of water?"

"Nope." His hooded eyes are trained on my lips as he speaks.

"Then what do you want, *Mr Woodgate?*"

He's so close now that his lips are tickling the shell of my ear.

"For you to call me Tyler while I'm buried deep inside you," he whispers.

I gasp, my insides doing a backflip at his words. I'm no Virgin Mary but I've never had a man talk dirty to me before. *It's exhilarating.*

"Where's your bedroom, Amanda?"

His voice is thick with seduction as he whispers in my ear. The tickle of his breath against the side of my neck has my skin prickling and my core throbbing.

I take Tyler by the hand and silently lead him through my small, mediocre house. *Is this really happening?* A sudden wave of insecurity threatens to swallow me whole as we start to walk up the stairs. *Why would a man like him be interested in a woman like me?* I nudge a pair of Ronan's abandoned football socks out of the way with my foot so that Tyler doesn't have to step over them. This all suddenly feels overwhelming, like a dream I've got no business having.

Tyler must sense my shift in mood because he stops me at the top of the stairs, gently spinning me to face him. With my face in his hands he gently rubs at my jaw with the pads of his thumbs. It's both comforting and possessive somehow.

"Are you sure this is what you want?" He looks me dead in the eyes, gauging my reaction, searching for any trace that I'm not fully on board with what's about to happen.

"Absolutely." I don't even hesitate, I don't need to. "It's just...been a long time."

"For you and me both," he admits, leaning in and planting a soft kiss on my lips. His admission makes me feel a little less nervous.

"It's this way." I indicate to the door on our left with my eyes and this time he picks up *my* hand and takes me into the bedroom.

Thankfully, it's tidy as I caught up with all the washing earlier. The curtains are slightly drawn but a sliver of moonlight makes it through, casting my sheets in a silvery glow. The vision of Tyler Woodgate standing in my bedroom has my mouth watering. In my small room, his presence is all the more imposing.

I sit on the edge of the bed and watch as Tyler undoes the buttons on the black shirt he's wearing and peels himself out of it. His broad chest is covered with a smattering of salt and pepper hair that matches his temples.

"God damn," I whisper to myself as he stalks towards me. There's no mistaking how turned on he is from the impressive bulge straining through his pinstripe trousers. *Maybe there is a God after all and I'm not on his shit list.* The man standing before me must be some next level divine intervention. This sort of thing doesn't happen to people like me.

"Are you ready for me, Amanda?"

Yes, Sir.

Chapter Ten

Tyler

I'm acting a lot bolder than I feel. The goddess in front of me deserves to be worshipped and I hope I can live up to my bravado. Truth be told, I'm nervous as hell. It's been a long time since I've been with a woman and Amanda isn't just any woman. She's sexy and sophisticated with some secret extra ingredient that I haven't managed to identify yet but it's there, calling to me like a siren song.

Amanda's chest rises and falls with anticipation as she watches me move towards her. She leans back on her arms and watches me intently. If she's nervous, she's hiding it well. Her shapely curves are accentuated in the shadows created by the moonlight and I'm torn between wanting to rush over there and rip her out of those clothes and slowly peeling back each layer, savouring every second.

I settle for option b as I reach the edge of the bed and she sits up to kiss my stomach. With her hands splayed across my abdomen, her vibrant red varnished nails work their way up to my chest, exploring as she goes. *It feels good to be touched.* I'd forgotten how good. Work has always kept me so busy but then Amanda stomped her way into my life in those goddamn heels and turned my world on its axis.

Reaching down I pull her sweatshirt up and over her head, revealing a simple black lace bra. It does nothing to contain the fullness of her tits as they spill out over the top. She studies my face for any sign of displeasure, the first sign of insecurity I've seen from her so far. She won't find any here. She's even lovelier than I imagined.

I kneel on the bed and climb over her forcing her backwards. She naturally parts her thighs to make way for me to lay in between them. Despite all the reasons why this is wrong, nothing has ever felt more right than the feel of her body pressed underneath mine.

"Has anyone ever told you how devastatingly beautiful you are?" I groan, running my hands over her fair skin.

"Can't say that they have."

Amanda's answer is flippant and off the cuff. She's preoccupied with curling her fingers in my hair and kissing my neck but I'm annoyed by her response. It's clear she hasn't been treated well in the past and has no idea of her true worth, something I plan on rectifying immediately.

"Well they should. Every day." My voice is a low murmur in her ear as I unclasp her bra and slide the straps down her arms.

I stop kissing her for a moment to simply appreciate the beauty laid out in front of me. She flutters her eyelashes shyly and looks away while my eyes leisurely peruse her bare breasts.

"Am I making you uncomfortable, Amanda?" I straddle her hips and sit up, waiting for her to meet my gaze.

"I'm just not used to being *seen*." She fidgets awkwardly beneath me, not sure where to put her arms as she partially covers herself.

I gently lift her arms and place them back down on the bed either side of her, exposing her once again.

"Well I see you, and I can't stop looking."

It's hard to tell in the semi-darkness but I'm sure I see her blush at my compliment.

"I'm going to strip you out of these leggings now and impale you with my cock."

"Good Lord!" She laughs in surprise. "Do you kiss your mother with that mouth?"

I grin at her, glad to have alleviated some of her anxiety. "My mother has been gone a long time so this mouth is all yours."

I make light work of discarding her leggings and undies on the floor at the foot of the bed before undoing my own belt and stepping out of what remains of my suit. Amanda's eyes widen at the sight of my tented black boxers. I couldn't hide how turned on I am right now even if I wanted to. And with the hungry way she's eyeing me up, I'm mighty glad I can't.

Amanda watches in silence as I hook my thumbs in the waistband of my boxers and lower them to the floor. A small gasp escapes her lips as I step towards her and kneel back on the bed in front of her.

"Damn it," I hiss, realising I've left my wallet in my jacket pocket which is still downstairs. "I don't have a-"

"It's OK," Amanda cuts me off. "I can't have any more children and I haven't been with anyone for...well, a really long time."

"It's been several years for me too." I confess, hoping to put her at ease. "I'm definitely clean."

"Then impale away," she laughs, throwing herself back onto the bed.

She's relaxing a little now and it's beautiful. The way her eyes crinkle at the sides ever so slightly when she laughs is fast becoming my favourite little Amanda-ism.

As I crawl up and over her, lining myself up between her legs, Amanda stops laughing and meets my eyes. It's deliciously intense the way she doesn't shy away from my eyes as I slide inside her smoothly. Her sharp intake of breath lets me know she's feeling suitably stretched by my intrusion.

"Tyler," she whispers, digging her scarlet nails into my shoulder blades.

"That's not even nearly loud enough," I barely recognise my own voice. It's all gravel and need. "I won't be satisfied until I hear you scream it."

Amanda grins and her eyes roll back in her head when I pump my hips harder, driving into her deeper. She arches off the bed forcing her tight nipples to brush against my chest. *Perfection.* Bending down, I suck one into my mouth and tease it with my tongue. Amanda whimpers and almost lifts off the bed. *How could I have been so worried about not having the stamina anymore?* With a creature as divine as Amanda wrapped around my cock, I could go all night.

The wooden slats of the bed groan beneath us from the strain, in perfect sync with the slam of the wooden headboard against the wall. Add that to the perfect moans falling from Amanda's lips and we've created one hell of a sinful cacophony. I do hope her neighbours aren't the prudish type because there's no way they can't hear us.

"Tyler!" She cries out, wrapping her legs around my hips.

"That's it baby, let me hear you." I roar, nailing her to the mattress.

"TYLER!" *And there it is.* The scream I was so desperately craving. I come undone inside her as she falls apart beneath me.

I lay on top of Amanda, careful not to crush her, stroking her hair and kissing her lips softly while we try to regain our breath.

"That was..." she pauses looking for the right word.

"If you say nice then I may have to leave here and jump off the nearest bridge." I chuckle breathlessly, rolling off of her onto my back beside her.

"Well we can't have that. I was going to say incredible."

"Incredible I can work with. I could definitely use that glass of water now though."

Amanda laughs and reaches for her robe hanging beside the bed.

"I'll go." I stop her gently with my hand. "I can't have you waiting on me after that show stopping experience."

Amanda smiles and I'm momentarily taken aback by how natural this all feels. I slide my boxers back on under Amanda's watchful gaze.

I pad down the stairs to the kitchen in the darkness and pour two glasses of water. I manage to find the hall light switch on my way back and admire all the family photos along the wall on my way back. So many happy childhood memories of the twins at varying ages. I can't help but notice the total absence of any man in any of the pictures. I think back to what Ronan said to me that day in my office about Amanda being sad and lonely. Kids are so perceptive, they don't miss a thing.

When I return to the bedroom, Amanda has gone from the bed but I can hear the shower running down the hall. I place the glasses down and strip back down to nothing before going to find her.

Sad and lonely isn't something she'll be experiencing again any time soon.

Chapter Eleven

Amanda

When I wake in the morning, I'm alone in the bed. *Shit.* My heart sinks. *Surely he wouldn't hit and run, would he?* I sit up, looking around for any sign as to whether or not he's still here. I can see his clothes are still strewn over the bedroom floor making me feel instantly better. Just as I'm about to get out of bed to find something to put on, the bedroom door opens and Tyler comes in holding two steaming mugs of coffee.

"Good morning beautiful," he smiles.

Jesus, who wakes up looking that good in the morning? His hair is all messed up in the most adorable way and he's wearing just his boxers. Suddenly feeling self-conscious in the cold light of day, I gather the bedding and pull it up higher around my chest to cover up.

Tyler frowns as he places the mugs on the dresser. "Don't cover up on my account."

I fidget and giggle nervously, "No one wants to see that in the daylight, trust me."

Tyler's beaming smile has now been replaced with a stern expression as he slides back into bed next to me and looks at me.

"Don't ever talk about yourself that way," he scolds. He brushes his fingertips along my jaw to my hair and buries his hand deep in its waves. "I saw every stunning inch of you last night and do you know what?"

I shake my head in response and try to look away but he doesn't let me.

"I fucking loved it," he whispers into my ear before kissing my neck gently.

I smile at his words but still can't help myself from indulging in my self-deprecating habits. "That was different, it was dark," I mutter as he continues his trail of gentle kisses.

He stops suddenly and looks up. "What exactly are you afraid of me seeing that I haven't already?"

"All my...flaws. I'm not as young and slim as I used to be, I've had two children." I figure I may as well tell him all my insecurities. He's not the kind of man who will let this go until I tell him anyway.

He unclenches my fingers from the bedsheets at my chest and lays me back down next to him with the sheet covering us both. He manoeuvres down the bed until he's laying between my legs with his head at my stomach, propped up on one arm.

"You're talking about this, right?" he asks as his fingertip traces the length of my caesarean scar.

I nod self-consciously, breathing in as much as I can to make my stomach as flat as possible, not that it's achieving much.

"You're worried I won't like this beautiful thin, silver line that brought your wonderful children into the world safely?"

I don't say anything, I just look at him in surprise. No one has ever said anything like that to me before.

"Well you're wrong," he says seductively before running his tongue along the length of my scar and kissing it. The intimacy of it sends shivers right through me. "Anything else?" he murmurs against my skin.

"All of it" I exclaim, waving a hand in the general direction of my wobbly thighs and bum.

Tyler's gaze darkens and smoulders. He pulls my legs apart suddenly, causing me to moan. "Do you know what the first thing I fantasised about was when you walked into my office?" He starts to kiss his way along my inner thigh and nips as he goes. "These legs wrapped around me. These stunningly sexy legs." He continues kissing my thighs and grips my hips firmly.

Regardless of what I think about myself, I can't deny how hot it is to see him looking up at me from between my legs. I run my fingers through his hair and start to relax into the sensation of his kisses, despite how exposed I feel in the harsh light of day. I begin moving my hips gently as his lips move closer to my most sensitive part.

"And as for this sweet, tight..." Tyler's looking at me like I'm his next meal when suddenly we hear the front door slam.

"Muuuum" I hear that dreaded word being called from downstairs. *Shit.* I look at Tyler in panic and he looks just as alarmed.

"I thought you said they weren't coming back until this afternoon?" Tyler whispers hurriedly and he jumps off me and scrambles for his clothes.

"They're not meant to be, Chloe said she would take them to Ronan's football game. Fuck, what are we going to do?" I ask out loud but not really expecting an answer. I throw on the nearest pair of jeans and a t-shirt, not bothering with underwear and am thankful to see that Tyler is also dressed in record time.

"Muuuum?" I hear again but louder this time as Ruby comes up the stairs.

"Just a minute darling!" I call out as I frantically scan my room looking for somewhere to hide a full grown man. My eyes settle on the space under the bed and Tyler looks at me in horror.

"You've got to be kidding me?!" he whispers.

"Have you got any better ideas?" I snap.

Tyler shakes his head and mutters something under his breath as he drops to the floor and shimmies underneath it. The last glimpse of him vanishes under the bed just as there's a knock at the door.

"Mum, what are you doing?" Ruby calls from the other side.

Satisfied that Tyler cannot be seen from the doorway I open the door to greet Ruby.

"Good morning darling, what are you doing home?" I put on my best smile and try to look relaxed.

Ruby looks at me suspiciously. "What happened to your hair?" I don't answer right away so she shrugs and carries on. "Chloe just stopped off so I could pick up my headphones," she shrugs casually. "Do you know where they are?"

I make a mental note to brutally murder my sister for this later as I walk with Ruby along to her bedroom to help look for her headphones. Once Ruby leaves again I hurry back to my bedroom to give Tyler the all clear.

"It's safe, she's gone." I tell him as I re-enter the room. Tyler's top half slides out from under the bed and he grins naughtily.

"That was way too close." I puff my cheeks out and rake my fingers through my wild hair.

Tyler nods in agreement as he wiggles out from under the bed. "I found this," he says, holding up last night's black lace bra and flings it at me. "Although looking at you in that t-shirt I much prefer you without."

I look down in horror to see that you can indeed see my nipples through the thin white material as Tyler hauls himself out from under the bed.

"I also found some other interesting things under there," he laughs as he pulls me in for a kiss.

"Oh yeah?," I cringe in embarrassment hoping he's not referring to my vibrator. He gives me a knowing grin. "It's been a while," I say by way of an explanation.

"Well not anymore." Tyler holds me close so I'm pressed up tightly against him and he kisses me deeply.

"We can't take risks like this again though," I say seriously. "That was a close call."

"I know," he nods and kisses the top of my head. "I meant what I said, let me take you to the lake house. No one will find us out there."

I snuggle into his chest and sigh, breathing him in. Deep down I know nothing good can come of this and it can't last. *How could it?* Yet I can't help but fall further down the rabbit hole.

After an hour or two of more sex and coffee, I let Tyler out the back door where he's less likely to be spotted and go indoors in search of my phone. *Twelve more missed calls.* I ignore them all and dial my sister.

"Why on earth did you let Ruby come back for her headphones?" I ask my sister by way of a greeting.

"Good morning lovely sister, thank you for looking after my children for me," she exaggerates what I should have said down the phone. "I figured you'd be awake so didn't see the big deal."

"Sorry, and thank you, but it almost *was* a big deal," I hiss. "It was almost a *very, big* bloody deal!"

"What are you...ohhhh," she drags the word out as realisation finally dawns. "You brought someone back didn't you?" I can sense her grinning from here.

"Not just *any* someone. Can the kids hear you?" Despite the seriousness of the situation I find myself grinning right along with her.

"No, they're way over there. Come on spill! Who was it?"

"Tyler Woodgate" I whisper into the phone, even though I'm home alone.

"Shut the fuck up!" she says louder than necessary. "The super hot headmaster?"

"Shhh! Keep your voice down! And yes."

"Well, I'll be damned, I'm proud of you girl! I need to know everything, obviously so I'll be round later once the kids are in bed for all the details. I'll bring wine."

Before I get a chance to respond she says "Got to go, Ronan's about to get a yellow card. Love you, bye!"

Chapter Twelve

Tyler

To say I'm distracted would be an understatement. Although it's the weekend, I have a stack of papers on the coffee table mocking me. I need to read these reports and email back my response but every time I try, my mind wanders back to last night.

Aside from the uncomfortable hard on that keeps distracting me, I'm also unbelievably tired. One sleepless night of sexual deviance and I'm an exhausted car crash the next day! *Who said getting older wasn't any fun?*

Huffing, I set the papers back down on the side and close my laptop, opting instead to put the kettle on again. I keep thinking about texting Amanda, but worry that it's too soon. I've never been very good at this sort of thing and now I'm seriously out of practice.

Fuck it. I take my phone out and type a quick message while the tea brews.

Thanks for last night. I promise not to ambush you at your house again. Sorry for any questions thrown up by Ruby.

I know I'm playing with fire. I could potentially lose my job if this gets out. I've never been one to disregard the rules but Amanda makes me throw the whole damn rule book out the window.

My phone beeps as I stir my tea.

Shame, turns out I quite enjoyed being ambushed by you. Maybe I'll ambush you next time.

Amanda's message reawakens the sleeping beast in my boxers. Apparently he didn't get the memo that we're tired today.

A knock at the door brings me out of my wayward thoughts. I chuckle heartily to myself as I go answer it, still thinking of all the ways I could respond.

"Top o' the mornin to ya big brother." Tom chirps as I open the door. He's always loved goofing around with accents and voices.

I check my wristwatch. It is still the morning, just about.

"You're very chipper this morning," I note as he walks past me into the house. "What are doing over this side of town?"

"I'm always chipper. I had a photography session with a lady a few streets away." Tom fidgets with his keys as he answers. A tell tale sign that there's more to this story than he's letting on.

I narrow my eyes and go in for the kill, pouring him a cup of tea as I do so to sweeten the deal. "What sort of shoot?"

"Just portraits." He shifts his weight from one leg to the other. Now I *know* he's lying.

"Spill the beans Tom Tom." *He hates it when I call him that.* "It was a boudoir shoot, wasn't it?"

"Yeah, but she's married."

"So?" You do those for women all the time to spice things up with their husbands. "What's the big deal?" I shrug, sliding his tea across the counter to him.

"The problem is I don't usually kiss them and their husbands aren't usually abusive a-holes." Tom slurps his tea, looking like he has the weight of the world on his shoulders.

"Damn. I didn't see that one coming." I ponder his predicament, secretly enjoying the opportunity to think about something other than my own hot mess.

"You and me both," he sighs. "He's a real piece of work, Tyler." I'm not used to seeing my jovial younger brother looking so forlorn.

"And by the look on your face, it wasn't just any kiss, right?" I pat my brother on the shoulder comfortingly.

"I fear not, big brother," he says dramatically. I swear he should have been on the stage instead of behind the lens. "Anyway, how goes the situation with the smoking hot parent?" Tom drinks his tea and grins at me like a maniac, shelving his own drama to talk about mine.

"Well, funny you should ask. I think I might have put my back out." I rub the bottom of my spine, not entirely joking.

Tom wolf whistles and folds his arms across his chest. A shit eating grin spreads across his face quicker than wildfire. "That good, eh? There's clearly life in the old dog yet," Tom teases.

"Except that today the old dog is tired and aches from head to toe. It seems the recovery process is somewhat longer than it used to be."

"Damn it Tyler, what were you doing, erotic acrobatics?" Tom laughs heartily as he drains the remainder of his tea. "And is the poor nameless woman alright? You didn't break her did you?" *Tom is finding this way too funny.*

"Her name is Amanda and no, she's fine. In fact I'd go as far as to say she's perfectly satisfied."

I try not to let the memories of last night linger in my mind. The last thing I need right now is a boner in front of my clown of a brother.

"Good for you, man. Listen, I've got to run, I've got another job at 1pm." Tom scoops up his keys and dumps his mug in my sink.

"Try not to ruin any more marriages!" I call after him as he sees himself out.

"Try not to break any more single mums!" *Dick.*

I pick up my phone and start to type my reply to Amanda.

Make sure you're wearing those heels. They'd look so good over my shoulders.

I smirk at my response and rearrange myself in my jeans. *I really need to do some work.* Sitting back down on the sofa, I try my hardest not to keep checking my phone for a reply but the temptation is hard to resist. Meeting Amanda seems to have made me regress by twenty years, rendering me a lovesick fool. It's been a long time since anyone's captured my attention the way Amanda has.

Three dots dance along my screen, taunting and teasing me with the promise of a reply but then it stops, only to start up again a few moments later. She can't know the torture she's putting me through, any normal person would not be sat here watching the screen like an idiot.

Eventually I'm put out of my misery:

The twins have camp in two weeks. I can come away with you then if that works? If you're sure that's what you want.

Oh baby, I'm sure. I can't think of a time when I've been more sure. The prospect of a whole, uninterrupted weekend alone with Amanda has me aching and hard all over again. I decide to run a cold shower to try and shake off my ever growing enthusiasm, but not before replying.

Perfect.

My plan fails epically as images of Amanda's thighs wrapped around me play through my mind. Her lips, her curves, her hair, all of them branded into my brain with the intensity of a hot iron. The events of last night play on a constant loop while the cold water pummels my neck and back. It's then I suddenly remember the phone call that started the whole evening off and an uneasiness settles in my stomach. With everything that followed, I'd almost forgotten the way she answered the phone. *She thought I was someone else. Someone sinister.*

I shut off the water and step out of the shower, wrapping a towel around me, lost in my own troubled thoughts. I have to know who she thought it was.

I almost forgot. Who did you think was calling you on the phone last night? You clearly didn't want to hear from whoever it was.

Amanda replies instantly this time.

Just the twin's dad decided to crawl out of the woodwork after all these years and start beating his chest, that's all. Nothing to worry about.

I frown as I read her words. You can't get a feel for someone's true feelings via a text message. My gut is telling me from the little I know so far that this guy very much *is* something to worry about.

The second that changes, I want to hear about it.

Now who's beating their chest? I roll my eyes at my overprotective response. I probably should've worded that better. Before I can overthink it, Amanda replies.

Yes, Sir.

And just like that, I'm hard all over again. *For fuck sake.* How is a man ever meant to get any work done?

Chapter Thirteen

Amanda

"Why are you in such a good mood?" Ruby mumbles as I vacuum in front of her TV show in the lounge.

"I'm always in a good mood." I smile cheerily. *I'm not exactly about to reveal the true reason why I'm floating on air today.*

"That's bullshit. No one is that happy doing the hoovering, especially not you. Stop being weird." Ruby arches her neck to see past me as she huffs and complains that I'm blocking her view.

"Mind your language." I tut, rolling my eyes. "I'm not being weird, I'm allowed to be happy."

"OK, cool. Can you mind out of the way now? She's about to dump him." Ruby ushers me out of the way just as a whole heap of teen angst starts gushing through the TV.

I roll my eyes and try to remember when it was that my children stopped seeing me as the centre of their universe and instead started acting like my very existence offends them. When Ruby was a baby, she used to twirl her pudgy little fingers around my stray strands of hair as she fell asleep in my arms. As a toddler, Ronan used to tell me he loved me three times every night before I was allowed to leave the room at bedtime. The memories make me smile. They may think they're all grown up and don't need me any more but they'll always be my babies.

I finish cleaning downstairs before heaving the vacuum cleaner up the stairs. By the time I get to the top, I'm out of breath and need to sit down. It's a wonder I managed to go as many rounds as I did with Tyler last night given my shocking lack of fitness and stamina. I make a mental note to check out the exercise classes at the leisure centre next time I take the twins swimming. I most definitely have an incentive to want to get in better shape now, despite Tyler's kind words about my wobbly bits.

If there were any doubts in my mind that Tyler wasn't sincere, they have been well and truly laid to rest by our text exchange this morning. Tyler hasn't stopped messaging since the minute he got home which is endearing. It's been a very long time since anyone has paid me any attention. I had started to accept my invisibility as part of motherhood but it's refreshing to learn that it doesn't have to be that way.

My phone vibrates in my pocket and I smile, ready for a smutty comeback from Tyler. Disappointingly, it's not from Tyler, it's Danny.

You can't ignore me forever.

Wanna bet? Arsehole. This will be his frustrated attempt to get a response out of me, seeing as I've ignored the fifteen calls he's already made to my phone this morning.

Why now? Why the sudden change of heart? As if the twins would even give him the time of day. They're not stupid, they know he treated us badly and that he hasn't bothered with them all these years. Even at the young age they were at the time, there was no disguising what was going on from them. Why on earth would they want to see him now?

I ignore his message, as I plan on doing with all his future attempts at contact. Thankfully due to the court ruling I don't have to give him the time of day and have no intention of doing so. Refusing to let him get to me, I leave my phone on the side and wheel the vacuum cleaner towards Ronan's room. I'm so preoccupied with Danny's message and Tyler's flirty conversation that I completely forget to knock before walking into Ronan's bedroom.

"MUUUM!" He yells, turning the brightest shade of scarlet I've ever seen on a human.

The source of his embarrassment is apparent by the tented blanket covering his lap amongst the array of tissues scattered across the bed.

"Jesus Christ Ronan!" I squeal, not knowing where to look. "What are you doing?" *Dumb question.*

"What does it look like? Get out!" Ronan screams, his hands flapping around frantically trying to find their way out from under the blanket. I've never seen him so flustered. If I wasn't so stunned myself, it would be hilarious.

"Sorry, sorry!" I hold my hands up in defence as I try to back away out of his room. Just as I'm about to leave, the sound of erotic moaning comes from his phone and fills the room.

"Is that porn?" I cry, putting my hands on my hips for the lack of anything better to do with them.

Ronan flaps about looking for his phone beneath the blanket, muttering a string of profanities under his breath and mumbling all the reasons why his life sucks and I'm the worst mother in the world.

"What's going on? I could hear shouting." Ruby bursts into the room unannounced, further adding to Ronan's humiliation.

Ruby takes one look at the scene in front of her and bursts out laughing. The sound accompanied by that of heavy breathing and screams of pleasure still coming from Ronan's phone.

"Fuck off Ruby!" Ronan shouts at her. "Fuck off the pair of you!"

Ronan finally locates the source of the porn and shuts it down while Ruby is doubled over laughing. Ronan picks up a pillow and launches it at Ruby's head but she rebounds it with her arm and it falls to the floor.

"Ew, gross! It's probably got your spunk on it. You're such an animal!" She screams.

"Right, that's enough! Ruby, out." I gesture towards the door, my expression leaving no room for doubt that I mean business.

Ruby slinks out of the door sniggering to herself. Once she's gone, I turn to face Ronan who's buried his face in the blanket and refusing to look at me.

"I'm sorry I didn't knock. I will make sure I do from now on. If you ever want to talk about...this," I wave my arm awkwardly in front of me. Not that he can see as he's still face down in the blanket.

"No Mum! Just get out!" He mumbles angrily from the blanket.

I decide to give him space and leave. Pushing him right now will only make things worse. Ruby is standing in her doorway with a smug look on her face.

"Not another word." I warn her sternly.

Abandoning the rest of the housework, I opt instead to make a cup of tea and sit down for five minutes. I stir the tea, contemplating how weird life is. The night before I was having the best sex of my life and feeling like a million dollars to then being thrown back into my crazy daily life that's like a bad episode of a soap opera.

Another message from Tyler has come through whilst I was upstairs.

It does things to me when you call me Sir. Things that it shouldn't.

I smile to myself, feeling rather satisfied that I can have such an effect on him. I'm just about to reply when the sound of screaming comes from the upstairs bathroom.

Running up the stairs two at a time, I make it on to the landing in record time and bang on the bathroom door.

"Ruby what's wrong?' I yell, so she can hear me from inside.

"I've just started my period!" She wails.

Jesus Christ. Take a deep breath Amanda. I lean my forehead against the door and close my eyes, counting to ten before I deal with today's next drama.

Ronan comes out of his room and walks past on his way downstairs. "Sucks to be you!" He shouts to Ruby as he strolls by, all traces of his humiliation gone now that the tables have turned.

Give me strength. I just stand there for a moment with my forehead against the bathroom door and my eyes closed, counting to ten in my head. *Why can't I just have a normal weekend like any other person?* Sometimes I try to remember what being bored feels like, it's such a distant memory these days.

"Muuuum, what do I do?" Ruby sobs from inside.

My phone vibrates from my pocket. Assuming it's probably Danny texting again, I'm ready to throw the damn thing out of the window. Thankfully it's just Chloe.

How's the rest of your weekend going?

You have no idea.

Chapter Fourteen

Tyler

"Here's your coffee, Mr Woodgate." Pam places down a steaming mug of black coffee on my desk, along with a whole stack of paperwork I'd rather not have to deal with.

Monday mornings are brutal. Especially when my mind is still elsewhere. Amanda and I spent the rest of the weekend messaging each other. My mind never wanders far from her these days.

"Thank you, Pam. How was your weekend?"

"Not as good as yours, it would seem." She gives me a sly smile, peering over her glasses at me.

"Pardon me?" I sip my coffee too soon and it burns on the way down.

"You haven't stopped smiling since you got here this morning. I raised four sons, I know that smile. It's the kind of smile only a woman can put on your face."

Before I'm given the chance to confirm or deny, Pam disappears out of my office with a chuckle, closing the door behind her. *That woman is far too perceptive.*

The entire morning is consumed by opening and answering emails. It takes until lunchtime just to clear my inbox. I don't have a meeting until 2pm which gives me a two hour window and an idea. Amanda mentioned some of her preferences and fantasies when we were messaging over the weekend and I'd love nothing more than to put some of them to the test with her.

I waste no time in looking up The Hammond Hotel where Amanda works and booking myself an immediate reservation online.

"I'm unavailable until my next meeting." I tell Pam on my way out. "Please take any messages and leave them on my desk."

"Of course Mr Woodgate. Everything alright?" She peers at me from behind her enormous stack of newsletters with concern.

"Everything's perfect." I grin with a genuine smile, feeling rather pleased with myself.

The air is crisp and cold despite the bright afternoon sun. Throwing my suit jacket on, I head to my car and make the short drive to the hotel.

Amanda's face is a picture when I casually stroll into reception carrying my briefcase. Her full, red lips part in shock as she watches me approach.

"What are you doing here?" She hisses under her breath, scanning the room for anyone that may have noticed us.

"You don't know me, we've never met." I tell her in a low, commanding voice that no one other than her would be able to hear.

There are only a handful of people here anyway, none of which are paying us any attention. The other receptionist is busy checking someone in and hasn't even looked my way once.

Amanda smirks and rolls her shoulders back, showing me her best customer service smile. "How can I be of assistance today, Sir?"

I try to ignore the ache in my balls, that will be dealt with soon enough.

"I have a reservation under the name of Seymour." I keep my face as straight as I can. "Seymour Butt."

Amanda slaps her hand over her mouth to stop the giggle that's threatening to erupt. She just about holds it together and keeps up our little charade.

"Ah yes," she smiles. "I've found you on the system. It was rather a short notice booking, I see." Amanda keeps her eyes firmly on her screen but her lips curve at the edges in a teasing grin.

"Something big and urgent came up." I reply, gesturing towards my trousers with my eyes.

This time Amanda has to cough to disguise her amusement and turns away to grab my room key.

When she's composed herself again, she turns back round and hands me the key.

"Here you go, Sir. Room 43. It's just up the stairs and to your left. I hope you have a lovely stay."

I place both elbows on the countertop and lean over towards her. She inhales sharply but holds her professional smile firmly in place.

"I'd like room service in five minutes. Please." I keep my voice low and authoritative.

"Of course Sir. Is there anything in particular I can get for you?" Amanda's eyes twinkle with excitement.

"I need something hot and wet." I all but whisper close to her ear. "I'm starving."

I swipe the key before pushing off the counter and walking away. I can almost feel Amanda's eyes on me as I walk away through the double doors towards the stairs.

This is complete and utter insanity. I have never done anything remotely like this in all my forty five years but somehow Amanda gives me the confidence to be the man I never realised I could be.

When I get to the room, I hang my jacket on the back of the door and go about closing all the curtains to set the right mood. I switch on a bedside lamp so there is just enough light to be able to see before stripping down to nothing. In the middle of the room is a huge four poster bed. It must be at least king size, maybe bigger. The white bed sheets are cold against my bare skin as I slide into the bed between them and sit against the headboard waiting for Amanda.

I try not to let myself think about how completely reckless this is while I'm sitting by myself in the darkness waiting. *Who does this sort of thing in the middle of the day when they're supposed to be at work?*

The sound of a delicate knock at the door, instantly chases away my worried thoughts, replacing them with anticipation.

"Room service." Amanda calls through the door.

"Come in."

Amanda swipes her key card with a beep and opens the door. The light coming from behind her in the corridor causes her to be completely silhouetted in the doorway. All I can see is the outline of her curves, her long legs and her heels. She's the complete embodiment of my every desire.

"Shut the door." I instruct from the bed.

Amanda does as I ask, throwing the room back into darkness. It takes a few moments for my eyes to readjust.

"So, you're turned on by my authority, is that right?" I ask, quoting one of her messages from the weekend. My voice is deep and commanding.

"Yes, Sir."

"And you want me to take charge?"

Amanda's bottom lip shines in the dim light from the lamp as she wets it with her tongue. "Yes please," she whispers on a breath.

The irony isn't lost on me that Amanda enjoys the illusion of me being in control and having power over her when really nothing could be further from the truth. I'm completely at her mercy, I have been ever since the day she walked into my office.

"I want you to come over here and stand beside the bed."

Amanda immediately does as she's told but chews on her bottom lip nervously.

"What if they notice I'm gone?" She looks at the door as if expecting someone to burst through it any minute.

"I've taken care of it. Now stop worrying and relax."

"OK," Amanda takes a deep breath and drops her shoulders.

"Good. Now take everything off except the heels...slowly."

Even in the semi-darkness I can tell Amanda is blushing but she follows my instructions, carefully untying her red silk scarf and letting it fall to the floor. Next is her blouse. With delicate fingers she undoes one button at a time, building the anticipation just like I asked. She looks down as she drops the blouse off her shoulders.

"Eyes on me Amanda." Even I'm surprised by how deep my voice sounds. I'm so turned on right now.

Amanda's eyes instantly flick back to mine and she gives me a teasing smile as she peels herself out of her blouse and drops it beside her. Her bra is black and sheer. I can see her nipples right through the opaque fabric. She's so goddamn sexy it physically hurts. When she unclips her bra, allowing her full tits to bounce free, I can't help but moan out loud at the sight. My reaction elicits a smile from Amanda and she continues with more confidence. The sound of her opening the zipper on the back of her pencil skirt is the only sound in the room. The tension is palpable as she finishes undressing, I can almost taste it in the air.

Amanda stands beside the bed in nothing but her shiny black shoes with the red glossy strap. I'm aware that time is of the essence today but it would be a crime not to take a moment to appreciate the beautiful sight in front of me. She really is breathtaking. I couldn't have made her more perfect if I had dreamt her up myself.

With bated breath, Amanda watches me admire her nakedness. If she's nervous or uncomfortable then she's hiding it well.

"What do you want me to do now, Sir?" Her voice is soft like a feather.

I throw back the bedsheets, uncovering myself and place my hands on my thighs. "I want you to come here."

Amanda inhales sharply as her eyes glide over my body. Without a word she kneels on the bed and crawls over to me, straddling my lap. I can feel her warm centre sliding over my hard cock as she settles over me. The sensation sends a ripple of pleasure straight to the pit of my stomach and I give her a sated smile. There is no better feeling on earth than Amanda's skin on mine. Her body connected to my body.

Amanda lifts herself off me just enough to hover over the tip of my cock. I manoeuvre slightly to tease her so that the silky head brushes around her opening. Before Amanda has the chance to sink herself onto me, I grip her arms gently, stopping her.

"You didn't think I was going to let you take charge did you?" I smile teasingly.

I flip Amanda off me and roll her onto the bed. She squeals at the sudden shock of being manhandled. "Bend over the bed." I bark. "Show me those pretty legs."

Amanda complies immediately with a flirtatious grin. Her perfectly globed cheeks taunting me from the edge of the bed. *Jesus Christ.* I don't know what I did to deserve this woman but I'm eternally grateful. The sight of her long, slender legs stretching from her high heels to her bare backside is enough to make my cock weep.

"You're so beautiful," I tell her as I stroke my fingertips up and down her legs making her shiver. I get off the bed and stand behind her, positioning myself in just the right place. Amanda moans softly in anticipation just as her phone lights up and starts to vibrate across the floor, making us both jump.

"Fuck, I'll just turn..." Amanda leans down to switch it off but stops midway. "It's the school."

Amanda picks up the phone and sits on the edge of the bed giving me a quizzical look. "Hello?" she answers. "Yes, this is Miss Wells."

I watch the colour drain from Amanda's face as she listens to whoever is on the other end of the phone. "Oh my god," she whispers. "I'll be right there." Amanda looks up at me with watery eyes.

"We have to go," Amanda starts hurriedly scooping up her clothes from the floor and putting them on.

"What is it? What's happened?" I ask, concerned. I reach out to touch Amanda's shoulder but she shrugs me off in her hurry to get dressed.

"Someone sent inappropriate images of Ruby around school and she's humiliated. Ronan saw them and trashed the Science lab." Amanda's speaking at a hundred miles an hour and getting dressed just as fast. "I'm such an idiot to think I could have any of this," she mutters to herself.

"Hey!" I stop her in her frantic tracks and pull her in, holding her close to my still bare chest. "We can fix this. What is all this?"

I feel my chest grow damp as tears start to fall from Amanda's eyes. "All of this," she waves her hand between her and I. "This sort of thing doesn't happen for people like me. I've been completely kidding myself. My life is at home with them," she sniffs.

I raise her chin with my forefinger so she has to look at me. "Listen, you're upset, understandably so. Let's go and put this right and talk about this again when things are calm. No rash decisions, eh?"

Amanda nods sadly and steps away, grabbing the last of her clothes. "Finish getting dressed, I'll see you at school."

Somehow when I get back to school I have to now fix a situation I'm meant to know nothing about. This is why I don't usually lie, lying always comes back to bite you on the arse.

Chapter Fifteen

Amanda

I can't believe this is happening. Why can't I just live a drama free existence? I march up to the school office as fast as these ridiculous shoes will allow. I don't know how I feel about any of it, it's completely overwhelming. I don't know what to think first, whether to be upset for Ruby, angry on her behalf, angry at Ronan, worried about the repercussions, proud of him for caring so much. I have no idea, I'm a swirling vortex of emotion right now.

Mr Foster, the Deputy Head is waiting for me at reception. He's a stern looking man, much older than Tyler. He has a portly stomach that overhangs his suit trousers and a moustache that reminds me of a boot brush.

"Thank you for coming so promptly." He greets me with a handshake.

I briefly nod and smile in acknowledgment. "Where are the twins?" I ask breathlessly from rushing over here.

"Right this way." Mr Foster leads me to Tyler's office, an ironic sense of dejavu washing over me. *This is nothing like previous visits to Tyler's office.* This feels ominous and impersonal somehow. *I wish Tyler was here.*

Ruby and Ronan instantly bring tears to my eyes. Ruby is curled up in a ball on a chair, hugging her knees. The mascara she's not meant to be wearing smeared down her pink cheeks. Ronan is pacing the room like an angry lion. He's so wound up that the tension rolls off him in waves. His knuckles are all bloodied and swollen from whatever inanimate object took the brunt of his anger.

"Mum!" Ruby wails, choking on a sob as she lunges off the chair, wrapping her arms around me.

"Ssshh, it's alright." I try to soothe her, stroking her long blonde hair.

"They're going to suspend me, Mum," Ronan blurts out frantically as he continues to pace up and down.

"Let's all just calm down and hear what Mr Foster has to say." I usher them both into the seats opposite Mr Foster, who is now seating himself in Tyler's chair. The action agitates me more than it should, he is the deputy after all, but it's not *his seat.*

"As you may already be aware, a rather unfortunate and unkind image of Ruby was distributed around the Year 9 pupils today via a social media app." Mr Foster is clearly uncomfortable about these images based on the way he shifts awkwardly in the chair that isn't his.

"But it wasn't me, Mum. Someone cut and pasted my face." Ruby interrupts.

"May I see the image?" I ask Mr Foster. Before he has the chance to reply, Ruby slides her mobile across the desk to me.

The image is of an extremely obese naked female body with Ruby's head superimposed on top. There's a flashing caption at the bottom that says 'Pigs like sex nearly as much as food.'

I gasp in horror at the cruelty some people are capable of. Not just people but children. *How can children be so awful to one another?*

"This is appalling," I say, looking up at Mr Foster. "Something has to be done about this. Look at her!" I cry, gesturing to Ruby who is sitting next to me, still sobbing her heart out.

"I can assure you, this matter will be dealt with swiftly and severely but there's also the serious issue of Ronan's actions." Mr Foster is a mask of indifference. He doesn't care one bit about what this will do to Ruby. All he's concerned about is his smashed up lab equipment.

"Ronan has a temper, yes. But can you blame him for feeling angry when he's just seen this happen to his sister?" I yell, struggling to contain my emotions.

"Please do not raise your voice at me, Miss Wells. Ronan has damaged hundreds, if not thousands of pounds of equipment today. That cannot go unmentioned."

"You're focusing on all the wrong things! I want to know how you're going to find out who did this to Ruby and what will be done about it." I'm so angry right now, I wouldn't be surprised if actual steam was coming from my ears. "If Mr Woodgate was here-"

"But he's not." Mr Foster raises an eyebrow at me and stares me down, daring me to challenge his authority.

I shut my mouth and breathe through my nose angrily. I daren't try to speak for fear of losing my temper completely.

"I'm going to recommend a cooling off period of two days for each of them." He says smugly, leaning back in the chair and smoothing his tie over his enormous stomach.

"What?!" I screech. "You can't be serious!"

"Oh but I am." He doesn't pause for breath as he launches into a speech about how the school has high standards to maintain.

I don't even hear the rest of his pompous, idiotic ranting. I just see red. The whole meeting escalates into chaos as I shout over him and nobody listens to anybody. Ruby cries even louder and Ronan jumps to my defence shouting louder than all of us.

"What is going on in here?" Tyler's authoritative voice of reason cuts through the room, silencing us all.

His dark eyes dart from me to Mr Foster, then the twins and back again, waiting for someone to offer him some sort of explanation.

"Miss Wells was just expressing her opinion on my decision." Mr Foster explains, breathless from raising his voice. He's still as red as a tomato which gives me a small sense of smug satisfaction that I managed to get under his skin.

"I can see that," Tyler replies calmly. "And what decision was that?"

"Ty-Mr Woodgate," I correct myself immediately but my slip up doesn't go unnoticed by Mr Foster, who narrows his eyes at me, assessing the situation. "The twins are being unfairly suspended."

"I see. Mr Foster, please explain what's happened in my absence so I'm all caught up."

Tyler sets his briefcase down on the desk and takes off his suit jacket as he listens. A jacket that less than an hour before was strewn across the hotel floor.

"An offensive image of Ruby was shared around Year 9 digitally. We have no idea who is responsible yet. I understand that this is very upsetting to all involved but Ronan took it upon himself to smash up Chemistry Lab 2 in response. I have merely suggested that the twins take some time out to cool off."

Interestingly, Mr Foster's whole demeanour has changed now that Tyler is here. His smug expression has been replaced with an earnest one that's trying too hard. He clearly knows his rank in the pecking order and my guess is he's less than pleased to have to take orders from Tyler.

"Call it what you like. They're being suspended. Mr Woodgate, please tell me you can see how unjustified it is to punish Ruby when she is the victim here and that Ronan was simply defending her. Albeit in the wrong way but still."

I look at Tyler pleadingly, willing him to make things right. He scratches at his beard, keeping his professional mask firmly in place. To watch this interaction from the outside you'd have no clue that he'd just watched me strip naked for him, baring everything to please him. The irony is I feel more bare and vulnerable standing here now than I ever did in the hotel.

"Given the situation and the clearly high levels of emotion involved, I'm inclined to agree that a cooling off period would be wise."

I gape at Tyler, unsure if I just heard him correctly. Angry tears pool in my eyes as Ruby wails even louder at his words and Ronan punches the wall.

"This is bullshit!" Ronan roars, making everyone else in the room jump. I'm too stunned to react, I simply stare at Tyler in shock as the tears spill over.

Ronan barges past Tyler, knocking his shoulder as he storms out of the room.

"Come on Ruby, let's go home." I whisper, holding out my hand to her, still not breaking eye contact with Tyler. "We're done here."

Chapter Sixteen

Tyler

"Is everything alright Mr Woodgate?" Pam asks, placing a fresh cup of coffee on my desk. "You look like you need this."

I've done nothing this afternoon other than reflect on how badly I handled things with Amanda and the twins.

"Thanks Pam, I've just got a lot on." I offer her a polite smile.

"You need to go and see that woman of yours after work. She'll put the smile right back on your face." Pam disappears out the door, closing it behind her. *If only that were the case.*

I fear I may have messed up so badly that she'll never forgive me. Somehow the feeling of guilt that I've failed Ruby and Ronan is even harder to bear than knowing that I've hurt Amanda. The whole situation is a shitshow.

I try calling Amanda again for the third time but she still won't take my calls. My eyes flick to the clock even though I only checked it less than a minute ago. *Just two more hours and I can go over there.* I had to cancel my 2pm meeting after what happened so that I could fill in all the necessary paperwork and ask Mr Foster to write his statement. *That man really is an arse.* If I had to guess, I'd say he had his nose put out of joint by me getting the Headship. He makes it his personal mission to make my life as difficult as possible.

Eventually the end of the day comes and I hot foot it straight over to Amanda's house to try and put things right with her as well as with Ruby and Ronan. I genuinely care about their welfare and it was hard to see them both so distressed today. Ronan has come a long way but an incident like that would test anyone's self control, let alone a pubescent boy with anger issues and a massive sense of duty.

I park the car up the road and walk the short distance to Amanda's front door. I know full well I could be seen but right now I don't very much care. *I have to fix this.*

No one answers the door when I ring the bell. I'm just about to walk away when Ruby opens the door, all puffy eyed and in her pyjamas.

"Hello Mr Woodgate," she says quietly with a sad expression. *The poor thing looks exhausted.*

"Ruby, how are you?" I give her a heartfelt smile.

"I'll be alright, thank you Sir." Ruby looks at the doormat and shifts uncomfortably. "Mum's just popped out."

"No problem. It's my fault for coming unannounced. I'll give her a telephone call instead." I do my best to hide my disappointment and make it seem like this was merely a courtesy call.

Just as I turn to walk back to my car, Ronan appears in the doorway beside Ruby. "Would you like to come in and wait, Sir? I make a wicked cup of tea."

I can't help but chuckle at him. There's something so likeable about these two. "I'd like that very much."

I follow the twins into the kitchen and take a seat at the table with Ruby as Ronan busies himself at the counter. A lot of clattering and banging comes from his general direction, making me smile.

"How's your hand, Ronan?" I call over the racket.

"It's alright. Nothing too bad." Ronan stops what he's doing and turns to face me. "I will pay back all the damage, Mr Woodgate. I'm sorry for losing my temper."

"Thank you Ronan, that's very admirable of you. It won't be necessary though. I've taken care of it. While I can't condone what you did, given the circumstances, I can certainly understand your anger."

Ronan gives me a small, understanding nod before going back to making the tea. "I hope you don't feel like I treated you unfairly earlier, Ruby. I of course want to support you in this and find out who did it. Please don't see your time off as a punishment in any way, I think some rest and space will be helpful for you."

Ruby keeps her eyes on the table but nods sadly. "I know, thank you Sir."

I'm about to go on when the sound of the front door diverts my attention. Amanda appears in the kitchen doorway wearing a grey fitted sweater and jeans, looking every bit as fierce as she did back in my office. It would seem that whilst the twins have had time to calm down, she has not.

"What are you doing here?" She asks, folding her arms across her chest.

"Mum!" Ruby scolds, embarrassed by her tone.

"It's alright Ruby. Your mum and I have some things to discuss if that's ok."

"No, actually, we don't." Amanda snaps. "Anything *the school* needs to make me aware of, you can put in an email."

With that, she marches off up the stairs and disappears. *Fuck. Now what?*

"Can you see Mr Woodgate out please, Ronan?" Amanda shouts down from upstairs.

"Oh for god sake," Ronan mutters, rolling his eyes. "I just made a really good cuppa."

Despite the awful situation I find myself in, I can't help but chuckle a deep throaty laugh at Ronan. "I'd like to have my tea first if that's alright." I reply. "It'd be rude not to after all the trouble you've gone to."

Ronan half-smiles which is about as much as you ever get from him, so I take it as a small win. He places the steaming mug down in front of me, the contents of which are like the colour of treacle. I've never seen tea quite like it. I resist the urge to grimace.

"Biscuit?" Ruby offers, sliding a Christmas tin across the table to me.

"Thank you." I smile in relief. Maybe I can soak up most of the tea with a HobNob. I dunk my selected biscuit in the tea and take a bite, even then the taste of the tea is so overpowering I almost cough.

"Mr Woodgate," Ronan sits down beside me so I'm sandwiched between him and Ruby. "Seeing as we're not in school right now, can I be honest with you about something?" His voice is a hushed whisper, presumably to stop Amanda from hearing.

"Of course Ronan, I always encourage honesty from students and the freedom to speak their mind." I sip my hideous tea while I wait for him to speak.

"OK, cool because the thing is, I know you're boning my mum."

I spit my mouthful of tea out, spraying it all over the table in front of me and almost choking to death in the process.

"Ronan, you can't say that!" Ruby hisses, looking at the doorway for any sign of Amanda while I try to regain some sort of composure.

"Well what would you have called it?" He snaps back, "Fucking? Shagging? Doing the nasty?"

I try to stop coughing and spluttering but Ronan's vast array of colourful vocabulary is certainly not helping my recovery. I imagine I'm the colour of beetroot from coughing fit.

"Ronan, stop it! You might kill Mr Woodgate, he can't breathe! You have to be careful with old people!"

Oh dear God. I try to mop up the tea with a cloth I found on the side as I clear my throat and try to breathe. Eventually, I recover enough to be able to speak. I don't even know which bit to address first.

"Thank you for your concern, Ruby. I'm not old enough just yet to be considered a choking hazard, but I appreciate the sentiment." I then turn to Ronan. "Ronan, you are quite right. I have been having an intimate relationship with your mother."

"See," Ruby hisses at Ronan. "The way *he* said it was much better. Way less gross."

"How do you both feel about that?" I ask, looking from one to the other to assess their reactions.

Ronan shrugs casually. "It's cool I guess. Mum's been much happier since, well until today when you pissed her off."

"Yes, that was rather unfortunate. I'm hoping to make amends. Ruby, what about you?"

"It's fine. I mean it's gross, but it's fine. We don't have to start calling you Dad or anything though, right?" Ruby screws up her face in the most amusing way.

"No, absolutely not," I chuckle. "You already have a dad."

"Fucking waste of space he is." Ronan mumbles.

I choose to ignore his colourful use of language and focus on the emotion behind it. "He's still your father."

"Nope. He's a selfish prick. He doesn't deserve to be called Dad."

Ronan is such a deeply intense character. I love peeling back his layers and seeing deeper. He's a very observant and insightful young man when he's not trashing things.

"And you're entitled to your opinion on that, Ronan." I notice Ruby's lack of engagement on the topic of their father. She's much more of a closed book.

"If it's alright with you two, I'd appreciate it if you kept my relationship with your mother to yourselves at school."

"There is no way we're telling anyone at school, Sir. Your secret is safe with us. Can you imagine how bullied we'd get?" Ronan makes a fair point.

"Well, if you're both sure you're OK then I best be off. I will try to patch things up with your mother when she's feeling more up to it."

Ruby and Ronan both say goodbye as I stand up from the table and head towards the front door. When I step into the hallway, Amanda is standing quietly just behind the door frame.

"How much of that did you hear?" I ask her quietly, pleased to see her expression has softened somewhat.

"I was here for the boning," Amanda tries not to smile but the corner of her lips curve up the tiniest amount as she averts her eyes to the floor.

"Ah, I see. The whole shabang. I really am sorry Amanda. Can we talk?" I reach out to touch her, but think better of it.

"Nothing comes before my children, Tyler. Not my job, not my friends and certainly not you." She makes her point abundantly clear.

"As well it shouldn't," I agree.

"Good night," is all she says before padding down the hallway in her fluffy socks and opening the front door to dismiss me.

I sigh defeated. "Good night, Amanda."

Chapter Seventeen

Amanda

"What? Why are you looking at me like that?" I close the door and turn to find the twins both watching me from the kitchen with judgemental looks on their faces.

"Bit harsh, don't you think?" Ruby comments, swinging on her chair in a way that irritates me daily.

"It's rude to eavesdrop." I tut, hoping to shut this conversation down before it begins.

"Like you did?" Ronan's tone is dripping with sarcasm. *Touché*. That kid is such a smartass.

"Fine, come on then." I sigh, flopping down on the chair next to Ruby. "You've obviously both got an opinion, so let's hear it. Although before we get to that, how, by the way, did you know about me and Ty-Mr Woodgate?"

Ronan rolls his eyes dramatically. "It was so obvious, Mum."

"It was?"

"Yup." Ruby chimes in, popping the p to make her point extra clear.

"Most Headteachers don't make home visits of an evening, drowning in aftershave and they definitely don't leave their ties under your bed." Ronan informs me.

"What were you doing under my bed?" It's not at all the point of this conversation but I want to know.

"Looking to see if you'd stashed any early Christmas presents." Ronan shrugs with a casual grin.

"It's not even November!" I squeal. "Anyway, we're getting off topic. You were telling me how harsh I am."

"You should at least talk to him." Ruby says matter of factly. "You can tell he's sorry."

"Who's sorry?" My sister asks, bundling through the back door carrying armfuls of carrier bags.

Great. This is all I need. A third person to join Team Tyler.

"Mr Woodgate." Ronan announces, stuffing his mouth full of crisps and dropping crumbs all over the kitchen floor.

"Aunt Chloe, tell Mum that Mr Woodgate deserves a second chance. He's all sorry and mopey without her." Ruby says, throwing her arms around Chloe's waist and squeezing her tight.

"Hold up, rewind. What's going on?" Chloe looks confused as she helps herself to a biscuit.

"I'll catch you up. Mum's been shagging Mr Woodgate and thought we didn't know, but then someone sent fake naked fat pictures of Ruby around school so I got angry and smashed up the Science lab. Mr Foster suspended us for two days and then *Mum* got mad but then when Mr Woodgate showed up, he backed up Mr Foster and Mum got *really mad.*"

Ronan has barely paused for breath this whole time and Chloe just looks blankly at him in total confusion. It's probably the most words Ronan's said at once for years.

"And then Mr Woodgate was just here trying to apologise and Mum wouldn't listen." Ruby adds.

Chloe takes a seat and puffs her cheeks out dramatically. "That's a lot of information for a Monday evening. Put the kettle on and start from the beginning."

• • • ● • ● • • • •

Thankfully the last few days have passed without incident. Ruby and Ronan had their 'cooling off' period and I suppose in a way, I had mine. I haven't spoken to

Tyler, I've ignored all his calls and messages but I have at least had time and space to think.

Being a parent means that you have to put your children first, above everything else. I think over all these years of doing it alone, I'm so used to fighting the world on their behalf that I don't know any other way. I'm all they've got so I've always protected them fiercely. I have no idea what it feels like to share the load and be able to think about what I want sometimes. Tyler was my first glimpse of that and I think deep down I feel like I don't deserve to have a special something of my own. The happy ever after has never been on the cards for me.

Danny continues to send threatening messages and call me incessantly. All of which I also ignore. Part of me thinks I should tell the kids, just so they can be aware in case he tries to approach them. He doesn't know our address but he's a smart man. He'll find a way to find us, it's only a matter of time. A reality that makes me feel physically sick.

"Mum?" Ruby taps me on the shoulder, dragging me out of my worrying train of thought. "You haven't forgotten it's the dance tomorrow night, have you?"

"No, darling. I remember. Drop you at Lucy's house for 7pm and collect you from school when you ring but park down the road so no one sees me." I recite her instructions from the other day.

Ruby smiles and breathes a sigh of relief. "Can you iron my dress, please?"

Funny how polite and civil they can be when they want something. "Yes of course. Bring it down and I'll do it later."

Ronan walks past on his way to the fridge buried deep inside a black hoody.

"What about you, Ronan? Are you going to the dance?"

Some incoherent mumbling comes from under his hood which I think resembles a 'maybe'. "Are you going with anyone special?"

"No."

I chuckle to myself because there was nothing incoherent about *that* response. "Do you want me to iron a shirt for you?"

Ronan shakes his head and disappears back to his room loaded with an armful of snacks. I have no idea where he puts it all. He's lean and thin but eats enough food for a small army.

The doorbell rings so I go answer it, pretty sure I'm not expecting any visitors or deliveries today. I open the door to the most enormous bouquet of brightly coloured roses and gerberas. It's so large that I can't even see the delivery man's face who's holding them.

"For Miss Amanda Wells," he says, thrusting the huge explosion of colour in my direction.

I thank him and wrestle the bouquet through the doorway, closing the door behind me. *I don't think I even have a vase big enough for all these!* Unable to see where I'm going through all the petals and foliage, I trip and stub my toe on a carrier bag of things that has been left in the hallway. "Ouch," I hiss.

"They're nice. Who are they from?" Ruby asks. "I bet it's Mr Woodgate."

"I don't know, I haven't found a card yet. More importantly, why is there a bag of stuff in the hallway? I nearly just broke my neck."

"Oh, that's Ronan's PlayStation. He's selling it to start paying Mr Woodgate back for the lab equipment."

I think my heart might burst. People can say what they want about my son. I myself have plenty to say about him, quite often, but he has a huge heart underneath it all. The fact that he's willing to sell his most prized possession to get back in Tyler's good graces and make amends is heart-warming.

Choked with emotion, I set the flowers down and start hunting through the leaves for a card. When I find and open it, it reads:

Dear Amanda,

I would never want to be your number 1, that slot has quite rightfully been filled by Ruby and Ronan. I would never dream of encroaching on that. But I sure would love to be all the numbers that follow after, if you'll let me.

Yours,
Tyler x

And that's all it takes to tip me over the edge. I sit at the kitchen table and cry like a baby. Ruby watches me completely bewildered by my response. Life is so rich with emotions, that sometimes they have to spill over so you don't burst.

"Are you going to forgive Mr Woodgate now?" Ruby asks quietly.

"Yes, I think that I might." I sniff.

Chapter Eighteen

Tyler

There is a thumping in my chest and a ringing in my ears that apparently passes as music these days. I have no idea what I'm listening to but it's certainly an assault on my senses. The school hall has been fully decorated in autumn themed decorations by the school council. Everywhere I look there are leaves and gold sparkles. It'll take weeks to get all the glitter out of the school. As much as I detest these occasions, it is nice to see the students have fun and let their hair down, although hopefully not too much.

I have persuaded as many staff as I could to stay behind and police the event. If past experience is anything to go by, there's always at least one fight, a few attempts at sneaking in booze and many emotional fallouts between the girls. Oh and not to mention the copious amounts of face sucking that I'm forced to bear witness to with way too much tongue action involved. *Maybe I'm just getting old.*

My thoughts have wandered to Amanda more than once while I've been patrolling the dance. I want nothing more than for her to forgive me. She won't return my calls or texts and it's killing me slowly from the inside out.

"Get down!" I shout, noticing a group of Year 8's trying to climb the lighting tower used by the drama department.

The boys are far too busy all laughing and egging each other on to hear me over the music so I have to shout even louder.

"Get down from there at once!"

This time they take notice and slowly climb down one by one, looking rather sheepish. *Did they honestly think they would go unnoticed hanging from the rafters like a bunch of wild apes?* "Sorry, Sir," they mumble.

"You can each deduct five merits on Monday morning. Off you go."

The boys all scarper as far away from me as possible. No doubt to go and find some other mischief that's out of my eyeline.

"Evening, Sir." A gentle voice comes from behind me.

I turn to see Ruby standing with a big smile on her face. She's all dressed up in a sparkly blue dress that matches her eyes and her hair is down and curled to one side.

"Ruby, you look lovely." I smile at her warmly. "How are you doing?"

"I'm much better thank you, Sir." She looks at the floor timidly.

"Good, I'm very pleased to hear that. And I'm glad you haven't let it stop you from coming tonight. Have a wonderful time."

I'm about to walk away and leave her to it when she says, "I liked your flowers by the way. They were a nice touch." Ruby flashes me a knowing smile.

"I'm glad you think so. Did they help?" I ask, hopefully.

"I'd like to think so. We're both rooting for you Mr Woodgate." Ruby smiles at me before heading off into the crowd to find her friends. The residual feeling I'm left with is warmth. Knowing that the twins feel that way means more than I could have ever imagined it would. They've both somehow managed to burrow their way into my heart and carve out a permanent place for themselves there alongside their mother.

I spot Ronan across the room looking smarter than I've ever seen him in a pair of dark jeans and a black shirt. His hair is gelled to perfection. It's so shiny that I can see it reflecting the disco lights from all the way over here. The sight of him makes me chuckle to myself. He's watching a girl from his class dancing with her friends. He's looking at her like a man who's walked the desert for days, looks at an oasis. *It's probably the same way I look at his mother.*

I casually make my way over to him, the whole while he doesn't take his eyes off her once.

"Why don't you ask her to dance?" I ask quietly, coming to stand beside him.

Now that I'm so close, the overpowering scent of his aftershave is tickling the back of my throat and making my eyes water.

"Na, she'll probably just laugh at me," he shrugs.

"Only one way to find out." I nudge his arm encouragingly and he gives me a wonky half smile.

"Na, seriously Sir, I'll just look like a bell- I mean idiot."

I stifle a chuckle at his slip up. He's the first kid I've ever overlooked bad language for. I just love how unapologetically Ronan he is.

"You know, when you're old and going grey, like me. You won't look back and regret most of the things you *did* do. You'll regret the things you *didn't*."

"Like sleeping with my mum?" He smirks.

"Watch it." We both smile at the floor, trying not to look like we're enjoying each other's company.

"So, do you have any advice then, Sir?" Ronan asks, gesturing over to the girl on the dance floor.

"God no! You've seen how terrible I am with women. You're mum won't even speak to me!"

Ronan laughs out loud, despite himself.

"You're on your own kid. I only said you should go for it. I never said I had any ideas on how."

Ronan walks away from me towards the girl with his hands shoved awkwardly in his pockets. I can still see his shoulders shaking in laughter from our exchange as he makes his way towards the group of girls. I need to walk away and do something else but I find myself watching because I'm rooting for him just as much as they're rooting for me. My heart's in my mouth as I watch him approach. I feel like I might choke on it at any given moment. My nerves are off the scale as I watch him speak to her. To my absolute relief she smiles and tucks her long dark hair behind her ear. Her cheeks turn the brightest shade of pink but she offers him her hand and he leads her out onto the dance floor. My heart swells with pride, so much so that it's in danger of bursting. I never had a son, but if I did, I like to think he'd be like Ronan. He might be reckless and impulsive, but he has a heart of gold and he is more resilient than most of the adults I know.

As they start to dance, I walk away, content that he's overcome that particular milestone without a hitch. I want to call Amanda and tell her all about it, but I know she won't answer. The thought saddens me as I check my watch to see how much longer I've got until I can crawl into bed in the peace and quiet.

"Mr Woodgate, can I have a quiet word?"

Great. Mr Foster. "Certainly," I say with forced cheerfulness.

When we step outside into the empty corridor, everything is much quieter which is a relief to my ears.

"I have written my statements about the unfortunate events of last week. Which one I submit, largely depends on you." He gives me a polite smile, but it's complete bullshit.

"Come again?"

"Well, you see, I have written two different statements. One of which outlines the events exactly as they happened and another that's somewhat more, shall we say, creative?" He smirks at me this time, no longer trying to hide his intent behind politeness.

I fold my arms across my chest, giving him full eye contact as I wait for him to explain himself.

"The thing is Tyler, we all know you're tapping Amanda Wells. I mean, I can't say I blame you, ten years ago I'd have banged her myself, she has got legs to die for." He raises his eyebrows and whistles to accentuate his disgusting point. I clamp my mouth shut, showing extreme restraint, even though I'm steaming fucking mad inside. I let him finish his speech, a speech he is clearly taking much glee in.

"Anyway, the point is, you don't get to have your cake and eat it too. You swooped in and stole this job from right out under my fucking nose. It should have been mine! You don't then get to bang the hot mamma too. So I'm evening the playing field."

"If you have a point, you best get to it really fast." I clench my teeth as I grind the words out.

"Put simply, one statement will put the whole thing to bed and you can go about your business, buuuut you have to kill your relationship with yummy mummy." He grins at me, revelling in his pathetic scheme. "The other statement means you get to keep the girl, assuming she'll still have you, but your career will be over. I've embellished that baby so well that you'll never get another job in a school again." He all but rubs his hands together as he paces about in front of me, enjoying his power trip.

"And the point of all this being what, exactly?" I rub my beard with my palm and cock my head to the side trying to figure this idiot out. If he was hoping to get a rise out of me, he's sadly mistaken.

"The point is," he roars, turning almost scarlet, "that you stole my job! So one way or another I will ruin you!"

Jealousy. Figures. He's so angry that I haven't taken the bait, it's laughable. If I wasn't such a professional then

I would currently be doubled over with laughter on the floor. Instead my calm facade stays firmly in place.

"Submit whichever statement you wish, Mr Foster. It's of no concern to me but if you ever dare to use Ruby or Ronan again to meddle in my affairs then you will be very sorry indeed."

I give him no time to respond. Turning my back on him, I march back into the dance hall, welcoming the thump of the music. *Anything is better than listening to that blithering idiot.*

Chapter Nineteen

Amanda

Whoever came up with the idea of appraisals in the workplace needs a swift slap to the face. *Why would I want to go and talk to my boss about my failings and dreams?* Most days I'm just thankful that me and the kids are all dressed and semi-functioning.

Today is my turn for this joyous, annual event. I glance at the clock noting that I've got precisely five minutes until the torture begins. With a heavy sigh I pick up a pen and notepad just in case and make my way down to the manager's office.

The manager, Michael, is fairly new. He only took over a few months back and I've had very little to do with him so far, thankfully. He's much younger than me and gives off major dickhead vibes. He's full of bullshit that he regurgitates out of some business textbook he probably read back in college.

"Amanda, come in," opens his door with an over-the-top smile.

I follow him into his office and take a seat opposite him at his desk.

"How are you? How have you been?" He asks enthusiastically as if he knows me and gives a damn. His pen is already poised to take notes.

"Fine. Thank you."

"Good, good," he says absentmindedly as he scribbles something down. "And how are the kids?"

I resist the urge to roll my eyes. He's clearly read my file. He doesn't give a crap about my kids, this is all such superficial bullshit.

"They're fine too. Thank you." I do my best to smile politely.

"Oh really? That's good, because I noticed you've been late for work quite a bit since September and wondered if there was an issue I need to be aware of?"

He stops writing and looks up at me, waiting for a response. I clench my teeth in irritation.

"No, no problem. Sorry about that, I do try my best."

Michael gives me a tight smile. "If you could try a bit harder on that one, that would be great. Punctuality is key."

I say nothing for fear of running my mouth off. Instead I nod and press my lips together. *Please let this be over soon.*

Michael goes through a whole string of pointless questions that I answer as politely as I can. The bottom line is, I don't really know what's gone well in the last six months or what I could have done better and I definitely don't care how I can grow as a team member. This is just something I have to do to pay the bills.

"I have one more question for you, then you'll be pleased to know that you're free to go. Where do you see yourself in five years? And is there anything we can do to help you achieve your professional goals?"

The temptation to laugh out loud at this one is really high. I have to swallow my amusement. *I mean, really?*

"To be perfectly honest, I don't have any professional goals. I'm quite happy as I am. I come to work, I do my job and I get paid. That's it for me."

Micheal looks at me like he just swallowed a bug. "That's not very ambitious of you, Amanda. Surely you want to achieve something for yourself?"

If I could spit flames at him right now, I would. *How dare he! Who does he think he is?*

"With respect, you don't know me. I have a very full and demanding life. I achieve what I need to. We can't all be climbers."

"I didn't mean to cause offence, Amanda. I apologise. Please keep up the good work." He can't get me out of his office quick enough.

I don't know if he was scared of what else I'd say if I carried on or if I'm just such a huge disappointment that I wasn't worth any more of his time. *Whatever*. It doesn't matter either way. I have no room in my life to think about my own dreams or ambitions. Deciding to let Tyler in has been a big enough leap of faith. I have to think for three people, not just one.

By the time I get home, I'm tired and ready to be done with the day. It took over an hour to pick up Ruby and Ronan from school because of roadworks and all they did was bicker the entire ride home.

"I'm ordering pizza tonight," I tell them as we all pile into the house. There's no way I'm cooking.

Obviously no one responds, they both disappear off to their rooms as I pick up all the letters from the mat and dump all the bags and coats in the hallway. I carry them through to the kitchen and put them on the side as I flick the kettle on.

I type out a quick message to Chloe.

Ordering pizza if you're interested.

Of course she's interested, she can smell pizza a mile away. Her reply is instant.

Be there in 5

I smile to myself as I pour us both a cup of tea. True to her word, Chloe appears through the back door five minutes later.

"Tough day?" She asks.

"What gave it away?" I ask, handing her a mug.

"Your face, your hair and the fact you're ordering pizza."

"What's wrong with my hair?"

"It's extra frizzy. That always means you're frazzled." Chloe shrugs and sips her tea.

I shake my head in amusement as I start opening the stack of letters. It's mostly the usual assortment of bills and boring grown up junk I'd rather not deal with.

"Forgiven the hot Headmaster yet?" Chloe enquires as casually as she can manage. I know she's desperate for any gossip though.

"Actually I have," I reply, distracted by the last letter in the pile. It doesn't look like a bill. This is a 'bad news envelope' as our dad used to call them. "I'm going to go and see him..." I trail off as I open the letter and start to read it.

"What's wrong?" Chloe asks, panicked. "You look like you've seen a ghost."

I ignore her, continuing to read as my eyes start to blur with tears.

"Mandy, what is it?" Chloe puts her hand on my arm.

"Danny's taking me back to court. He wants the kids." I whisper the words so Ruby and Ronan don't hear and because if I say it too loud it might make it real. "This can't be happening." I mutter in disbelief.

"OK, don't panic," Chloe says calmly. "You know he won't win. He's a freaking psychopath Amanda. No one in their right mind would give him access to the children."

"But what if they do? What if he's lawyered up and wins them over? You know how convincing he can be! He's the best liar I've ever met. What if he gets custody and I lose them? I can't let them go to him, Chloe, I can't!" The words just keep tumbling out as my mind spirals into a frenzied panic. My worst nightmare is coming true and I don't know what to do first.

"Breathe, Amanda," she soothes, wrapping me up in a hug. "It won't come to that, I promise."

"I wish I had your confidence."

"You're a good mum, sis. Anyone with a brain will be able to see that. It's all going to be fine."

I hope she's right.

Chapter Twenty

Tyler

Half-term can't come soon enough. So much has happened during my first term here that I'm exhausted. I'm not used to this level of drama in my life. Just a few more days and I'll be getting out of here for a while. My plans of taking Amanda to the lake house are nothing more than a pipe dream now. She's made it clear she wants nothing more to do with me. A hard truth that hurts me way more than I'd like to admit.

Mr Foster has no idea how pointless his pathetic threats are. There is no relationship with Amanda to save. I must sigh out loud without realising it because Pam stops doing the filing and looks up.

"Everything ok?" She gives me a warm smile. She's got such a comforting, maternal way about her.

"Hmm. Can I ask you something?"

"Of course, fire away."

"Have you heard any rumours going around school about me?" I lean back in my chair and take my glasses off, rubbing my eyes.

Pam chuckles softly and puts down her papers. "This is a school, Mr Woodgate. The only thing that spreads faster here than gossip is germs. Not that I pay it any mind. People's business is their own."

I suppose she's right. You're not privy to the gossip when you're at the top of the chain so it's easy to forget how prevalent it is.

"Anything in particular you're worrying about?" Pam enquires.

"What rumours are going around about myself and Amanda Wells?" *I'm not entirely sure I want to know the answer but I've said it now.*

"It's not really a rumour if it's true is it?"

Touché. I raise an amused eyebrow at her. "That's a fair point."

"There is plenty of speculation about your relationship with Miss Wells. You're not as discreet as you think you are." Now it's her turn to look amused.

"Yes, well it's mostly a moot point now. It would seem it's over before it began." I tell her sadly.

"Ah, I did wonder as much. You've not had your usual spark these past few days." Pam gives me a sympathetic look and presses her lips together. "For what it's worth, I think you'd be perfect together."

Me too.

• • • ● ● • ● • • •

When the end of the day finally comes, I pack up my briefcase and head down the corridor towards the staff car park. I glance out the window at the girls' netball club that's in full swing down below, stopping dead in my tracks to do a double take. *Is that? It can't be.*

I squint and move closer to the window, thankfully no one else is around because I must look like a right perv. I know that full curvy figure and those long soft curls even at this distance. I can't quite believe what my eyes are telling me. Amanda is playing netball in the shortest netball skirt I think I've ever seen and the t-shirt hugs her chest in a way that shouldn't be legal. I can't decide whether I'm more angry or aroused, I seem to be a generous helping of both.

Abandoning my plans to get home, I march down the stairs and out onto the netball court. The game instantly grinds to a halt as the girls all stop and stare, wondering who I'm making a beeline for.

"Miss Wells, can I have a word? Please?" I add, attempting not to sound as tightly wound as I feel.

Amanda nods obligingly and excuses herself from the game, following me into the empty changing block.

"What do you think you're doing?" I snap, once I'm sure we're out of earshot.

Now that she's so close, I can see her skin glistening with a sheen of sweat and she's slightly out of breath, only adding to the appeal.

"Helping out with extracurricular activities as requested by your Head of PE. We had a letter about it last week and I thought it would be nice to spend time with Ruby," she explains, all wide eyed and innocent, acting as if I was born yesterday.

"In that?" I fold my arms across my chest and try not to look down.

"It's a netball uniform," she challenges back, also crossing her arms so we are both in a standoff.

"Yes I can see that, but it's entirely inappropriate. What sort of message are you sending the girls?" The more she defies me, the more turned on I become. It's utterly absurd.

"First of all, it's no different to what the rest of the team are wearing and -"

"The rest of the team are kids!" I hiss, trying hard not to raise my voice in case we're heard. "You're a woman, my wo-"

We're interrupted by the sound of chatter as a group of girls comes into the changing rooms to get their bags. I pull Amanda backwards into a cubicle and slide the lock. I hold her there with her back pressed to my front as we wait. She's still breathing heavily from playing netball, or maybe now the reason has shifted to the situation we find ourselves in. Either way, I place my finger over her lips and my hand on her chest to try and quieten her breathing and slow the rapid rise and fall of her chest.

We listen as the girls chat about this and that, giggling and messing about right outside the door. The air in the tiny confines of the cubicle is thick with tension. We're both trying to hold our breath so as not to give ourselves away but being crushed against her looking like a wet dream, that's no mean feat. If I were to be found like this by a student, it would be the end of my career. *What was she thinking turning up here like this?*

Amanda remains silent but her heart is beating wildly in her chest against my forearm. I grip her tightly against me and if I'm not mistaken she's pressing backwards into me enjoying the contact.

Slowly and silently she turns in my arms to face me. The space is so tiny that we're practically nose to nose. Amanda looks at me with an unreadable expression while we continue to wait. I honestly have no idea what she's thinking or feeling right now. All I know is I've missed her and I want her so badly.

Eventually the sound of giggly chatter fades and the door bangs shut, leaving us alone again in our silent confinements.

"Tell me what you want Amanda," I whisper, my lips almost touching hers. I search her eyes desperately for the answer.

"I want you to finish your sentence."

"What sentence?"

"The one you started before we got interrupted." Her voice is so quiet that if we weren't so close it'd be inaudible.

"Amanda, listen. I'm sorry about what happened, I-"

"I want to be your woman." She whispers against my lips.

I freeze, unsure if I heard her correctly. Every cell in my body is humming with anticipation at the closeness of her.

"Tell me it's not too late," she adds, wrapping her arms around my shoulders and losing her fingertips in my hair.

I don't answer her with words, my body takes over as our lips meld together. Everything I want to say, I show her instead with a kiss. I pour all my feelings into it, many of which I can't even name myself yet. I just know that when we're together everything feels right.

Amanda tightens her grip on my hair and I weave my arms around her waist. I'm acutely aware of all the places our bodies are touching and the temptation to peel her out of this skimpy outfit is unbearable. But I can't, not here. This was a close enough call as it is.

"Come away with me next week like we planned. Please." I'm willing to beg at this point, if that's what it takes. I want so much more.

"Yes."

Chapter Twenty-One

Amanda

The smile on my face is uncontrollable as I watch the trees whip past the windows on our drive through the countryside. I've worked hard to put all thoughts of Danny and court aside so I can focus on things with Tyler. According to Tyler's sat nav we are only a few minutes away from the lake house. I've never been on a weekend away with a man before. In fact, I've never been on a weekend away at all. There's never been money left over for luxuries such as this. I feel like an overexcited child on the way to the toy shop.

Tyler squeezes my thigh gently as he indicates and turns into a gated driveway between the neatly manicured hedgerow. His hand has only left its place on my leg to change gear, other than that Tyler has been in physical contact with me the entire time. I can't deny that it feels good. The heat of his palm travelling up my leg and sending a thrill of excitement through me is addictive.

The house comes into view at the end of the driveway on top of the hill. I can already tell that this place must have spectacular views from where it's situated. It's a beautifully traditional English country house with a thatched roof and external wooden beams. The front door looks like it should be hanging on a Medieval castle with its wrought iron fixings and huge gargoyle knocker. As the name would suggest, there is a large lake to the side of the house that sparkles in the sunlight as we park up. There's a cool breeze in the air that rustles through the bulrushes lining the lake, making the most calming sound.

"This is stunning," I tell Tyler, as he takes my hand and walks with me towards the house.

"Wait until you see inside." He flashes me a handsome smile that nearly takes my breath away. The closer we've gotten to the house, the more relaxed and care-free he's become. Being away from work suits him almost as much as being in charge. *Almost.*

Tyler proudly gives me the grand tour of the house. Each room is such a unique blend of country charm and grand opulence. The living room in particular grabs my attention with it's deep pile fur rug on the floor in front of the open fireplace. There's no fire lit there yet but my mind is busy conjuring up all the things I'm hoping Tyler will do to me in front of it. My cheeks flush at my train of thought and I'm suddenly in a hurry for the tour to be over. That is until we step into the master bedroom.

"What do you think?" He asks, seeming to genuinely seek my approval.

"Wow."

I'm completely spellbound. I've never even stayed in a hotel as fancy as this. The bedroom is enormous with large floor to ceiling windows on three of the walls giving a wrap around view of the lake and gardens. As predicted, you can see for miles. When I manage to tear my eyes away from the view, the room itself is just as breathtaking. A huge, wooden four-poster bed is in the centre with lush velvety drapes that hang around it. Either side are more thick fur rugs like the one downstairs and a set of deer antlers hang on the wall. To the side there's a doorway leading to an en-suite and on the opposite side is a wardrobe big enough to live in.

Tyler chuckles as I continue to gape at my surroundings. "How about I get the bags while you make yourself at home? Be right back."

After a swift kiss on the forehead, Tyler leaves me alone. It's so quiet here that I can just about hear his shoes crunch on the gravel outside. I let out a contented sigh. *I could get used to this.* The thought immediately makes me panic, filling me with feelings of guilt at being away from the twins. *What is it about mothers that makes us forever in need of a break but then the moment we get one we feel guilty about having it?*

I'm so lost in my own head that I don't notice Tyler come back until his arms wrap around me from behind and pull me against his chest.

"Glass of wine?" I feel his lips jostle my hair as he speaks.

"Mmmm, yes please."

• • • ● • ● • • •

The next few hours fly by in a relaxed haze. Things feel different here, as if all the tension has melted away and we can just be us. We've laughed and drank unknown amounts of expensive wine. Tyler has fed me bread and cheeses that I've never even heard of. Some of which I enjoyed, some of them made me want to throw up which only made us laugh harder. I feel like I've fallen through a portal into another world. This couldn't be any further from my life. *My real life.* Part of me feels like I could wake up at any moment and realise I'm simply dreaming.

In my experience, anything that seems too good to be true, usually is.

I try hard to fight off the rising feelings of self-doubt. They seem to slowly creep up on me when I'm not looking. The wine will be fuelling my spiralling thought process and I try hard to suppress it. The nagging voice in my head telling me I'm not good enough is never far away, it likes to pop up at moments like this and spoil everything. Although, I can honestly say I've never had a moment like this before. Being here with Tyler is something I've never even dared to dream about.

"Fancy going for a walk?" Tyler asks when the current wine bottle runs dry.

Despite the cold Autumnal air outside, I do think some fresh air would help cut through the wine induced haze and straighten my thoughts out. "Sounds great."

Tyler leans in and cups my face in his hand, running the pad of his thumb along my jawline and across my bottom lip. He leans in and kisses me softly. His touch is so soft and gentle, a stark contrast to our previous interactions. It's comforting to know that there's more here than just primal attraction.

My bottom lip hums from the delicate feel of Tyler's tongue dancing along it. I lean closer and wrap my arms around him, craving the closeness between us.

"Come on," Tyler sighs against my lips. "Before I change my mind."

Tyler slides his hand into mine and pulls me up off the sofa. Once we are suitably wrapped up in coats and scarves we make our way outside hand in hand towards the lake. As we walk, Tyler tells me tales of how he and Tom used to try and catch fish in the lake but usually caught nothing other than pondweed or a cold. The stories of him and his brother are heartwarming, Tom sounds like such a character. Their childhood seems idyllic, like something out of a children's book.

"When did your parents pass?" I ask, hoping not to dampen the mood but wanting to get to know him better.

"Dad went about eight years ago. Died in his sleep, which was as peaceful as you could hope for. Mum sadly had to spend her last few years in a dementia home and she followed him five years after." Tyler looks out over the rippling water, a far away expression in his eyes.

I snuggle into his side and squeeze his hand tightly.

"Tom and I couldn't bear to sell the house so we kept it and did it up. We both come here often to escape."

"I can see why," I whisper.

We let the next few moments pass in silence as we watch the setting sun reflect on the water. The oranges and reds look as if they're melting into the lake.

"About what happened..." Tyler turns to me and starts to explain.

"You did the right thing." I interrupt. "I overreacted and I'm sorry."

Tyler gives me a puzzled look as he sweeps the wild strands of hair away that have blown across my face.

"I'm so used to fighting for them that I don't know any other way. It's been this way for so long, it's a hard habit to break." I look out at the trees, not wanting to meet his eyes. Talking about myself makes me feel self-conscious and awkward.

Tyler gently tilts my face back to him with his hand. "I want you to know that this is so much more to me than just sex, Amanda. And you don't have to fight alone anymore, if that's what you want."

Tyler's words and the sincerity of his expression make my eyes blurry with tears. No one has ever wanted me before, much less all of us.

"We're a lot to handle." I joke, trying to hold back the tears.

"Good job I've got big hands," he grins, waving them at me to make his point.

I laugh out loud and pull him in for a kiss. He knows just the right things to say and how to lighten the mood.

"Any chance those hands know how to make a fire?" I tease, shivering a little from the cold.

"You're in luck. I'm like a real-life caveman." Tyler flexes his biceps under his coat and beats his chest. "Me make fire."

With a giggle and a rising feeling of excitement, I follow Tyler into the house. *Maybe a happy ending could be on the cards for me after all.*

Chapter Twenty-Two

Tyler

Amanda looks good here, as if she were always meant to be here, in this house with me. I watch her take her boots off and hang her coat on the rack like she's lived here all her life. Her cheeks and nose are pink from the cold and her hair is tousled. I'm dying to rake my fingers through it and get tangled up in her but I promised myself I'd be a gentleman this weekend and that is exactly what I'll do. *No funny business until the time is right.*

"Are you hungry? I was going to cook us some dinner." I offer, walking towards the kitchen.

"What happened to man making fire?" She teases, coming up behind me and wrapping her arms around my chest.

"I can do both." I turn in her arms and lift her up so her legs are wrapped around me too. "I'm a man of many talents."

"Yes, I remember," she whispers,

watching my lips as if they're the only thing in the world she needs. "How about I go and change into something more comfortable while you start that fire?"

Amanda's eyes blaze with desire and it takes all my willpower to put her down so she can go to the bedroom. I watch her curvy hips sway down the hallway until she turns the corner and then set about lighting the fire.

By the time Amanda returns, the fire is roaring and the beef is roasting in the oven, filling the kitchen with a mouth-watering aroma. Not as mouth-watering as the sight of her so-called 'comfortable outfit. She slinks into the kitchen wearing a matching black satin camisole and pyjama bottoms with a lace edge. Her hair is damp from the shower and spills over one shoulder, causing her skin to break out in goosebumps.

"I don't have a hairdryer," she says, wrapping her arms around herself to cover up how cold she is.

"Come and sit in front of the fire." I hand Amanda a new glass of wine and lead her by the hand to the fireplace.

I sit on the rug facing the open flames and pat the space between my legs for her to come and join me. Amanda leans back into my chest and sighs contentedly as she sips her wine and watches the flames dance.

I'm acutely aware that Amanda is wearing nothing under that slip of satin and that she's pushing against my growing erection on purpose. I gently run a trail of kisses across her exposed shoulder and she shivers, letting out a quiet moan.

"Tyler," she whispers, closing her eyes and leaning her head back against me. "I've missed you."

"I've missed you too, beautiful." I can't resist anymore, I fist my hand in her long hair and tilt her mouth towards mine. Capturing her bottom lip between my teeth, I kiss her with urgency. Our tongues and lips eager to reunite and come together again. I manoeuvre her round so she's beneath me on the rug. She sinks into the thick fur and looks up at me with a lust-filled gaze. *Fuck me, she's so beautiful.*

Slowly I slide her silk bottoms down and discard them next to us, exposing her milky thighs and the ever watchful snake tattoo that sits poised at the apex.

Amanda stares deep into my eyes as she slowly parts her knees and opens her legs for me. The glow of the fire dances along her bare skin making her all the more enticing as she opens herself up to me.

A deep moan rumbles in my throat at the sight of her. I wet my lips as I drink in the visual. I'm so ready to be with this woman in every way possible.

I lower myself between her thighs and grip her legs tightly. My tongue delicately traces her centre from bottom to top and Amanda arches off the rug with a gasp. I flatten and flutter my tongue against her hot core as she writhes around in the fur. Her hands grab my hair and tug at the roots almost painfully, but I don't care. She's so lost in pleasure right now, she's completely unaware that I'm watching her through the valley of her breasts.

"Tyler," she breathes, pressing herself into my mouth. "You're incredible."

Her heavy breathing spurs me on further and I lap harder and faster at her soft folds.

Amanda's thighs tighten around my head signalling that she's getting close. I suck gently on her sensitive bud causing her to buck beneath me and cry out. I smile into her and repeat the action again until she comes undone at my lips and I taste her on my tongue.

Amanda gasps for air and her legs fall loose either side of my head as she comes down from her orgasmic high.

"... on fire." I only catch the end of her sentence as I lift my head from between her legs.

"Mmm, yeah baby. Did you enjoy that?" I lean down towards her hoping to continue things further.

"No, I mean dinner! I think it's burning!"

"Shit!" I jump up off the floor and dash out to the kitchen. I was so caught up in what I was doing, I hadn't even noticed the god awful burning smell.

Grabbing the oven gloves, I open the door to be hit in the face with a plume of smoke. The fumes make me cough as I attempt to waft away the smoke with my gloved hands to see the damage. I pull out the oven tray displaying the charred remains of our dinner. The sound of Amanda's laughter floats through the smoke-filled air.

"Maybe that was one talent too many at once," she laughs, coughing on the smoke.

"In my defence, you distracted me with your sexy legs and your lack of underwear." I put the tray in the sink and run the cold tap over it. The tray hisses in protest and steam rises into the air.

"Is that so?" I turn around to see Amana lift her camisole up and over her head, exposing her full, round breasts. "How about we skip dinner and I distract you some more upstairs?"

My cock throbs painfully in my trousers. I've never wanted to accept an invitation more than this one. "Consider me distracted."

Amanda turns and disappears towards the bedroom with me hot on her heels. I shed my t-shirt along the way and within seconds of reaching the bedroom we are both completely naked, entwined on the bed.

"I have so much I want to say to you." I gaze down at her from where I rest on my elbows above her.

"Don't say anything," she whispers. "Show me."

Gently nudging her legs apart with my knees, I slide slowly inside her, never looking away from her eyes. *She needs to feel this. She needs to understand how much she means to me.*

Amanda grips my arms with her fingernails and looks back at me intensely. I bury myself slowly but deeply as far as I can before drawing back out just as slowly. This is not to be rushed. This isn't about sex or fucking, we've done plenty of that. This is the true meaning of making love. This is to show her how I truly feel by physically pouring all of my feelings into her.

For the rest of the evening, I make love to Amanda in my bed until we're both so spent that we fall asleep with me still inside her. I drift to sleep smiling, feeling a closeness and contentment that I've never had with anyone else before.

Chapter Twenty-Three

Amanda

"What was that?" I wake with a start and sit bolt upright in the bed.

There's a banging and crashing coming from downstairs that has my heart thumping in my chest. "Tyler, wake up!"

I shake his shoulder and he starts to stir. "What's wrong?" He yawns.

"There's someone downstairs!"

Tyler sits up and listens, immediately hearing what I'm hearing. "Stay here," he says, climbing out of bed in search of his boxers.

"No way. I'm coming with you. I'm not staying here on my own! " I slip on my pyjamas and wait while Tyler rummages through the wardrobe.

My eyes are glued to the bedroom door as I listen to the commotion downstairs, although it's hard to hear over the sound of my heart beating. Adrenaline courses through my veins as Tyler produces a baseball bat from the wardrobe and takes my hand.

"Stay behind me."

I nod and do as he says, too scared to do anything else. We creep through the house and down the stairs in the darkness, me tucked behind Tyler. I'm gripping his hand so hard, it's a wonder he has any blood left in it at all. The crashing and banging seems to be coming from the kitchen and grows louder with each step we take.

When we reach the kitchen doorway, Tyler stands in front of me blocking me from whoever or whatever is going there. I feel him raise the bat and I hold my breath and screw my eyes up tight just as he flicks the light switch. *Maybe this is how I die.*

"Tom?" I hear Tyler screech.

I open my eyes and Tyler drops the bat on the floor with a clunk.

"Oh hey Tyler!"

Tyler steps forward and I move to stand beside him, my eyes bugging out at the scene before us.

Tyler's brother Tom is dressed in a rubber Batman suit, although the mask is lying discarded on the floor and he's balls deep in a girl wearing a burlesque outfit who's bent over the kitchen table.

My mouth falls open in surprise and I can't help the giggle that escapes.

"You must be Amanda," Tom smiles at me and he's exactly how Tyler described him. You can tell from the way his dimples pop that he's the cheeky one. "I'm Tom, this is Emily."

The poor burlesque girl gives me a little wave from the table but buries her head in her layers of skirt with embarrassment.

"Well this is awkward," Tyler chuckles. "We'll give you a few minutes to, uh, do whatever you need to and then we'll start introductions over again."

"Sounds like a plan, Batman." Tom gives us a cheeky salute. "Wait, no, *I'm* Batman."

I giggle uncontrollably as Tyler bundles me out of the kitchen and shuts the door behind us. He turns the lights on and we shuffle into the lounge.

"I'm so sorry about that. Tom is...well he's Tom."

Tyler sits in the big leather armchair and I climb into his lap. "I hope they've been to a party," I laugh.

"Who knows with my brother. There could be any number of crazy explanations."

I wrap my arms around Tyler and cuddle close, still laughing at the absurdity of it all. I feel much better now that my heart rate has returned to normal and I'm not worried I'm about to die. "I'm just thankful you weren't being broken into by a crazy nut job."

"That's debatable." Tyler jokes, kissing me on the forehead.

The lounge door swings open and Tom strolls in, still in his full rubber Batman suit, complete with fake muscles. Emily follows behind holding his hand, her dress all put back in the right places now. Her cheeks are bright red with embarrassment and she can barely look at us as they come in and sit down.

"Sorry for the interruption, folks. I didn't know you were here." Tom smiles warmly as he takes a seat on the sofa with Emily. He doesn't look the least bit embarrassed by what we just saw but Emily is horrified enough for the both of them.

"Clearly." Tyler smirks. "Was my car parked outside not a clue?"

"I've had a few too many to be honest," Tom chuckles. "We fell out of the Uber and I didn't take much notice."

"It's nice to meet you Tom and Emily," I smile, trying to make poor Emily feel a little more at ease.

"You too." Tom sticks out his hand for me and shakes mine enthusiastically. "I've heard a lot about you."

"Likewise," I grin.

"Dare I ask why you're dressed like that?" Tyler rubs at his beard as he waits for Tom to reply.

"I took Emily to a photography launch party. Thought it was fancy dress, turns out it wasn't."

Tyler and I both burst out laughing. Even Emily chuckles nervously.

"Well, this was entirely unexpected for everyone involved." Tyler grins. "We're going to get some sleep so we can try and erase the image of you dressed in rubber with your junk out. See you party people in the morning."

Tyler ushers me out of the lounge and down the hallway. I trip up the stairs, barely able to contain my giggles.

"Poor Emily, she looks absolutely horrified," I whisper.

"So would you if you'd been railed by my brother dressed as a superhero."

"Don't be unkind," I swat at Tyler's chest as we make it make to bed.

"I'm not joking, that image is forever burned in my retinas."

Tyler shudders and smirks as he pulls back the covers for me to hop back into bed. Once we're both wrapped up in the thick duvet, Tyler pulls me into his chest and we drift back off to sleep.

• • • ● ● • ● • • •

"Morning sunshine," Tyler greets Tom when he eventually staggers into the kitchen looking worse for wear.

Tom nods and mumbles something incoherent, his eyes barely even open as he takes the mug of coffee that Tyler hands him. We've been up for hours making pancakes and enjoying them on the veranda. Despite the distinct lack of sleep last night, I've never felt more relaxed and refreshed. Tyler rubs soothing circles along my thigh as we finish our coffee, exchanging sniggers and giggles like a pair of school kids. Tom is completely oblivious to us, I'm not convinced he's fully conscious as I peer at him from over the newspaper we're pretending to read. He's slumped across the wooden garden table with his face pressed into the slats, hugging his mug like it's his lifeline.

"Is Emily ok?" I try to resurrect Tom from his hungover state.

"I'm not sure," he mumbles into the table. "I seem to be in the dog house."

"I can't think why." Tyler snips with a stifled half-smile.

Tom sits up, making me want to laugh even more. He has stripe marks all down one side of his face where he's been lying against the wood. "Help me man. How do I make it up to her?"

"You are a lost cause little brother." Tyler casually sips the last of his coffee.

I roll my eyes at their silly antics. There's no denying Tom is a character, and was almost certainly a handful in his younger years but I can't help feeling sorry for him. He has an endearing quality similar to a lost puppy that makes me want to help him. Unlike Tyler who is enjoying this far too much, sat smugly behind his newspaper.

"Why don't you make her breakfast? I saw eggs and bacon in the fridge." I try to think of things that I might appreciate in this situation.

Tom gags at my words. "Oh god, no, I can't. I'll be sick."

"Ok, why don't you run her a nice bubble bath?"

Tom smiles and stands up a little too quickly, having to steady himself on the edge of the table. "What a great idea! This one's a keeper," he points towards me and winks at Tyler.

"I know," Tyler replies, giving me a heartfelt look. Tom isn't listening, he's already back inside the house, undoubtedly on a search for bubble bath. "Amanda, there's something I've been wanting to tell you-"

Tyler is interrupted by the sound of my phone vibrating across the table.

"I'm so sorry, it's Ruby." I say, glancing down at the screen.

Tyler nods, understanding.

"Hi darling, everything alright? How's camp?"

"Mum, I think I have malaria," Ruby announces dramatically down the phone without so much as a hello.

I roll my eyes and shake my head, safe in the knowledge that she can't see me right now. "And what makes you think you have malaria?" I ask as seriously as I can manage.

Tyler's shoulders shake in amusement next to me.

I listen for the next five minutes while Ruby rambles and wails about a bunch of red, itchy gnat bites that she's acquired and how the cream doesn't work and her skin will never be the same again and she'll probably have to have a skin graft up her legs to cover the scars. *Honestly, I've never heard such ridiculous nonsense.*

I make the mistake of asking, "Do you think maybe you're being a bit dramatic?" A question I immediately regret asking because she then launches into another long speech about how I don't understand her and I never take her seriously. Eventually she pauses for breath and I manage to get a word in.

"Ruby, I will be collecting you and Ronan in less than three hours. If you can just manage to survive and hold on until then, you've got the rest of the day to tell me all the ways in which I've ruined your life. Ok?"

"Yeah, ok. Bye Mum," is all I get before she hangs up.

Tyler is grinning in amusement beside me. "Kids, eh?"

"Hmmm, indeed. Do we have to go back?" He knows I'm only joking. I miss the pair of them really, despite their Oscar worthy dramatics.

"Believe me, if I could steal you away and keep you here forever, I would. Sadly, duty calls for both of us."

I smile because I know he means it. When he talks about forever, I honestly think that he is sincere. I squeeze his hand and kisses the tip of my nose.

"Now let's get you home so you can call a plastic surgeon for Ruby."

Chapter Twenty-Four

Tyler

The ride home is a quiet one. We're both a little sad that the weekend is over so soon. When you get a taste of what life could be like, it's hard to give it up again. Our normal daily lives are so hectic and stressful in their own ways that it was nice to exist in our own bubble, just for a little while.

I nearly told Amanda that I love her but the phone rang and I haven't found the right moment again since. Or maybe I've lost my nerve and that's just a convenient excuse.

I pull up outside Amanda's house and we both sit in silence, not ready to get out of the car and accept that the weekend is over. The silence isn't awkward, just sad. Eventually Amanda leans down to undo her seat belt but I reach over and stop her.

"I love you," I blurt out, in the most unromantic way imaginable. *Smooth, real smooth.* Fortunately my blunt delivery doesn't seem to have ruined the message.

Amanda looks at me with a glassy-eyed smile. "I love you too." She throws her arms around my neck and we make out like a pair of horny teenagers in the front of my car for several minutes before reluctantly separating to go inside.

I grab the bags from the back while Amanda goes on ahead. The car door slams shut just as I hear Amanda cry out from inside. I rush inside with the bags to see what's wrong, abandoning them in the hallway on route. The crunch of broken glass beneath my shoes gives me a pretty good idea as to what's happened. Amanda is standing in the kitchen with her head in her hands crying at the devastation.

The back door has been smashed with considerable force given how far the glass has travelled. The room has been completely trashed, all the drawers and cupboards doors are hanging open and the contents strewn all over the place.

I pull Amanda into me and she buries her face into my chest, sobbing. "Sshh, it's going to be OK. I'll call the police and we'll get this sorted out." I do my best to comfort her as I stroke her hair. Truth is I'm angry, really fucking angry. *Who would do such a thing?* It then dawns on me that I should check the rest of the house, just in case the intruder hasn't left.

"I'll be right back. I'm going to check the rest of the house."

"Take me with you," she sniffs. "Please don't leave me on my own."

"OK " I nod, lifting her face up and wiping her tears away with my thumbs. I slip my hand into her and we crunch through the debris to the lounge.

The lounge is the same, only worse. Someone has slashed the sofa so all the stuffing is hanging out and every picture frame is lying smashed face down on the ground. Tears stream down Amanda's face as she looks at the mess.

"This is our home," she whispers sadly. "I worked so hard for all of this."

I have no words, I'm utterly devastated on her behalf and angry as hell. Amanda bends down to pick up one of the picture frames while I get my phone out to call the police.

"Oh my god!" She wails, dropping the frame on the floor like it just electrocuted her.

"What's wrong? Did you cut yourself?" I reach for her hands to check for injuries, instead I can feel her hands shaking in mine.

"The twins. Their pictures have gone." Amanda picks up another frame off the floor while I pick up the one she just dropped. Both frames are completely empty behind the broken glass, whatever photographs were inside them have been removed.

"Who would do this?" What's happened here feels personal. Someone has gone to a lot of trouble to cause as much destruction and hurt as possible.

Amanda doesn't reply, instead she runs off up the stairs whispering something to herself about baby stuff. When I catch her up, she's in her bedroom on her knees frantically pulling boxes and bags out from under her bed. A quick glance round tells me that no room has been spared. Amanda's bedding is shredded and all the things on her dressing table have been smashed.

Crouching down behind her, I gently put my hand on her shoulder so as not to startle her. I can feel her whole body shaking through my palm.

"What are you looking for?" I ask softly.

"Their baby memory boxes. They're gone. He's taken everything that's theirs." Amanda is so distraught, it's hard to watch. She rocks on her knees, tugging at her hair as she tries to breathe.

"Who did?" I gently take her hands away from her hair and drag her onto my lap on the floor where she breaks down into chest heaving sobs. "Talk to me, baby. Who did this?"

"My ex husband, Danny. The twins' dad." Amanda just about manages to get the words out, she's struggling to catch her breath through her tears.

"Breathe, Amanda," I rub her back in big slow circles and try to get her to take some deep breaths. "It's going to be OK." I rest my chin on top of her head as she cries, tucking her in under my arm.

Eventually she manages to calm down and regain control of her breathing. "There's so much I need to tell you," she whispers. "He's taking me back to court. He wants the twins!"

She looks up at me with big, sad eyes as more tears spill over and roll down her face. I don't think I've felt this heartbroken for another person before.

"Why didn't you tell me?"

"I didn't want to spoil things. I finally had something good in my life."

I take a tissue out of a tissue box that's been tossed on the floor and dab at Amanda's face. Her eyes are all swollen from crying and her nose and cheeks are pink.

"You still do. I'm not going anywhere, I promise. He won't win in court. Especially not after a stunt like this."

We just sit for a few moments huddled up on the floor together as Amanda processes the shock of what's happened. When she's regained her composure and is no longer shaking she leans up and kisses me on the cheek. "I'm ready to phone the police now."

"OK, let's go and sit downstairs. I'll go and pick up the twins from camp while you speak to the police."

Amanda smiles and squeezes my hand. "Are you sure?"

"Absolutely. And when you're done with the police, you're all coming to stay with me for a while."

"Oh no, I couldn't possibly ask-."

"You didn't." I interrupt. "I'm offering. Please don't argue. I need to know that you're all safe." *Because I love you.* I finish in my head what I can't say out loud. Now is not the right time.

• • • ● ●•● ● • •

I pull up at the camp lodge where Ruby and Ronan have been for the weekend. I can see them both sitting on the front step of the cabin with the organiser, their rucksacks and sleeping bags rolled up on the ground beside them. With everything that's happened, I'm late and they're obviously the last two to be collected.

"I'm so sorry I'm late." I tell the man in charge who doesn't look that much older than Ruby and Ronan.

"What are you doing here? Where's Mum?" Ronan asks. They both look surprised to see me, understandably.

"Your Mum's alright. There's been a bit of a problem. I'll explain in the car."

"Do you know this man?" The organiser asks them. He may look about fifteen but I'm glad to see he has some awareness around safeguarding at least.

"Yeah, he's Mum's boyfriend," Ronan says at the exact same time that Ruby says "Yeah, he's our Headteacher."

The young man looks utterly confused.

"Both of those statements are true." I chuckle. "Are you ready to go?" I ask the twins. They both look shattered.

They nod and pick up their stuff, following me to the car. They chuck their bags in the boot and climb in the backseats.

"I'm starving," Ronan mutters as I pull away.

"I'm sure I can fix that. We can stop on the way home for something." I look at them both in the rearview mirror. They're worried but don't want to say as much.

"Why didn't Mum pick us up?" Ruby asks.

"Your Mum's had a bit of a shock. Your house was broken into over the weekend and it's a real mess. It's quite shocking so prepare yourselves for the mess. We don't know exactly what's been taken yet. Your Mum's at the house with the police now, which is why she couldn't come."

Both twins sit quietly while they think about what I just said.

"Do they know who did it?" Ronan eventually asks.

"Not sure yet," I lie, unsure about what Amanda wants them to know. "I thought you guys could all come stay with me for a few days until things get cleaned up. How would you feel about that?"

Ruby shrugs and nods, seemingly OK with the idea.

"Do you have WiFi?" Ronan asks.

"Yes," I laugh out loud.
"OK, cool. Sounds good."

Chapter Twenty-Five

Tyler

It's been just over a week since Amanda and the twins came to stay. Living with teenagers is certainly an experience but one that I wouldn't change for the world. Although I do miss the use of my bathroom. I've barely had more than a few minutes in there this week in between Ruby's long showers and Ronan doing his hair every five minutes. I've never seen so many different hair products, my bathroom cabinet is like a salon!

"Good morning," Amanda rolls over beside me in bed and smiles.

Now this I could get used to. I don't ever want this to stop being the way I start the day. She's stunning even when she first wakes up.

"Why are you already working?" She pouts.

I'm sitting up in bed on my laptop, going through some statistics for a meeting later today. I take off my reading glasses and chuckle. "Busy day, lots to do."

"Too busy for this?" She asks, running her hand up my thigh beneath the bed covers and placing it over my awakening cock.

I close my eyes and tip my head back, enjoying the feel of her hand on me. "Never," I groan. I put the laptop on the floor so it doesn't restrict my growing erection. Amanda rubs her palm up and down the length of me, watching my reaction. She's laying beside me propped up on her elbow. The thin satin strap of her camisole has slid off her shoulder and the sight of her full tits spilling out is enough for me to be fully hard.

"How about you come and nestle those perfect tits around my cock?" I whisper in a gravelly voice.

Amanda's pupils blow wide but she gives me a sexy smirk. "Yes, Sir." I still don't think she's used to the dirty talk, but I like watching her reaction. I love that I can still shock her from time to time.

Amanda stays under the covers but slides over me, lying between my legs. I lean back against the headboard and watch as she lowers her pink satin top, baring herself to me.

I can't help the groan that rumbles deep in my throat. I'm so aroused right now, it's ridiculous. Amanda settles herself between my legs and slides my cock between her deep cleavage, still gripping the base tightly.

"Fuck," I hiss.

Amanda smiles, proud that she's pleasing me and starts to pump her hand hard and fast up and down the length of me. The action makes her tits jiggle and bounce around my cock. *Fuck me.* I'm going to last all of thirty seconds at this rate. This is way too hot for this time of the morning. "Amanda'" I whisper, gripping her long hair in my hand.

"Come for me, Sir," she looks up at me with a sexy half smile as she pumps harder and that's it, I'm done. I spill my load over her as I do my best to keep quiet.

If it weren't for the fact I've got to be in work in less than an hour and the twins are down the hallway, I'd extend this into a morning sex session in the shower.

Instead, I watch Amanda saunter into the ensuite to clean up in just a pair of satin shorts. She blows me a kiss over her shoulder as she goes.

"See you tonight."

I don't ever want her to leave. It scares me how quickly and easily I've come to that conclusion. I truly don't want her to go home. I want to wake up to her every morning and fall asleep beside her every night. Whether she feels the same is another matter. She's been through a horrible ordeal so now isn't exactly the right time to be making life changing decisions. I roll out of bed with a sigh. *That's a train of thought I will need to come back to another time.*

• • • ● ● • ● • • •

When I arrive at work, Pam already has a hot cup of coffee on my desk and a smile on her face.

"Good morning," she greets chirpily. "You look much better."

"Morning," I grin back, genuinely unable to stop the smile from spreading across my face. "I feel great."

"I'm very pleased to hear that because you've got a busy day ahead," she comments, handing me a wadge of sticky notes with various things I need to deal with on them.

I groan quietly to myself, I can feel my happy bubble popping already.

"You might want to hold on to those happy thoughts because Mr Foster is waiting to see you."

I rub my temples and take a large swig of coffee. *Wonderful.* "Please send him in."

Pam gives me a small, knowing smile and nods on her way out. I've never told her that I think Mr Foster is a complete and utter imbecile but I probably don't need to. Pam is very intuitive and almost certainly thinks the same. She's an excellent judge of character.

"Good morning Mr Foster, what can I do for you?" I get straight to the point as he enters and takes a seat.

"I was wondering if you'd given any more thought to our conversation at the dance the other night?" His lips curve up into a subtle, arrogant smirk.

"If you're referring to your attempt to blackmail and threaten me then no. I can honestly say that I haven't given it another thought."

His face momentarily falls with disappointment. *Predictable.* He's a typical bully and out to provoke a reaction. His frustration at not getting one is laughable.

"I'm going to assume by now that you've submitted your statement?" I continue, not giving him the opportunity to speak. "Which one you gave is of no concern to me."

"But some of the things I wrote there could end your career," he sneers.

"Then so be it," I sigh, growing tired of this conversation already. "What will be, will be, Mr Foster. Now is there anything else? I'm incredibly busy as I currently still have a job, as do you. I'm assuming you have classes to teach?"

Mr Foster runs his tongue over his top teeth in annoyance and shoves his hands in his trouser pockets as he stands to leave. He leaves without saying another word, closing my office door harder than is necessary. *Idiot.*

I'd be lying if I said I wasn't worried about the content of his statement. Who knows what bullshit he's made up. I certainly wasn't going to give him the satisfaction of thinking he's gotten to me. The one hope I'm holding on to is that I've seen his creative writing skills and they're not all that so with any luck his statement will be full of holes. The other problem he's going to have is that he will need proof of whatever he's claiming which he's unlikely to have given that most of it is going to be complete and utter bollocks.

I finish my cup of coffee, while I go through my emails, putting thoughts of Mr Foster to the back of my mind. I refuse to let him kill my Amanda induced buzz. I've decided to take Amanda and the twins out for dinner tonight. They don't know yet, it's a surprise. Hopefully Ruby and Ronan won't find being seen out with me in public too torturous. I don't want to hide away anymore. We are an *us* now and we haven't done anything wrong. (Aside from getting hot and heavy on school grounds.) That *was* a blatant rule break.

I check my phone to see if Amanda's been in touch but there are no messages yet. She was going to her house today to start cleaning up with her sister. Part of me wishes I'd told her she didn't have to, that she can stay with me. I'm just not sure if now's the right time to say something like that. She might not be ready to hear it. *Maybe I'll broach the subject over dinner and see how it goes down.*

Satisfied with my new plan, I leave my office to start the day's run of back to back meetings. By the time I return to my office for a quick bit of lunch, there is a message from Amanda asking me if the twins are ok. She's never checked in with me about them at school before. I'm not sure what has her worried today. Understandably, she might just be feeling on edge because she's back at the house.

I take a wander down the corridor to see if I can find them. They would have finished their lunch break and be back in lessons by now. It doesn't take too long, I can see Ruby from the upstairs window playing tennis with an amusing scowl on her face. From what her teachers tell me, Ruby is not a fan of PE unless it's netball. I chuckle and carry on walking in search of Ronan. I eventually find him in the Chemistry lab wearing his lab coat and goggles. I peek through the window but don't go in. He looks like he'd rather be anywhere else but here right now and keeps checking his hair in the glass. He catches sight of me through the window and gives me a small nod of acknowledgement. He'd never go as far as to smile at me in front of his friends. That would be like committing social suicide apparently.

I report back to Amanda so she knows all is well before going to my next meeting. The meeting is long and boring and goes on for far longer than is necessary. I'm pretty sure most of what's covered could have been sent in an email but instead I'm here being tortured with yet another pointless Powerpoint presentation.

Several hours in and there's a quiet knock at the door. Pam pokes her head around the door and apologises for interrupting. "Please can I have a quiet word with Mr Woodgate. It's urgent I'm afraid."

Pam wouldnt interrupt me unless it was absolutely necessary. I get up and leave the room to speak to her quietly in the corridor. "What's wrong?" My brow furrows in concern.

"There's a lot of commotion at the school gate. One of the students came to report there's a man outside bothering Ruby Wells"

My blood runs cold as her words sink in. "Call the police and send as many teaching staff out there as you can to round up the students. I'll deal with Ruby."

I hurry out of the school as fast as I can in the direction of the gate. *It has to be Danny.*

Chapter Twenty-Six

Amanda

Something isn't right. I can feel it. I've had an uneasiness in the pit of my stomach all day.

Are Ruby and Ronan OK?

I text Tyler just to make sure. I'm probably being paranoid which could be forgiven in light of recent events.

As far as I'm aware. Why do you ask?

I feel like a bit of an idiot now I've asked him. Obviously, Tyler has no idea what Ruby and Ronan are up to most of the time, they are two students among thousands.

Not sure. Don't worry, forget I said anything.

I stick a smiley face on the end to try and seem less weird, chuckling to myself as I send it. *I'm just being stupid.* Knowing that they haven't yet arrested Danny is doing crazy things to my brain. I know it was him and I know he's still out there. What's worse, is that he clearly knows where we are. The notion makes me feel sick every time I think about it. Apparently there's not enough evidence, or so the last officer I spoke to said. Seems he was pretty smart about leaving no tangible evidence behind. The police are aware of our history and my fears and are 'monitoring it'. *Whatever the hell that means.*

Fifteen minutes or so later, my phone pings with a new message from Tyler.

Just been to check and Ronan is in Science looking like he might drop dead of boredom and Ruby is in PE looking equally as unimpressed. Everything is normal.

Despite being home alone, I laugh out loud when I read Tyler's message. He's so sweet for checking even though I had no valid reason to ask. It makes me feel a little better knowing that they are both being their moody selves and everything is business as usual.

I'm not sure this really feels like home anymore. It's been tainted by Danny now. I'm at the house attempting to clear up the mess now that the police have finished here, but that's all it is, *a house*. The kids and I have settled in so well at Tyler's that the thought of leaving and coming back here fills me with dread and sadness. I don't want to outstay our welcome though, or come across as a freeloader. Which is why I'm here today making an effort to straighten things up.

I've booked a glazier to come and repair the back door, who should be arriving any moment and also a security company to install an alarm system. I can't afford this kind of hi-tech wizardry but Tyler insisted and is paying for it. Another reason why I think that he doesn't see our current living arrangements as a permanent thing.

Chloe is on her way over. She wouldn't take no for an answer when I said I was coming to clean up. I didn't tell her for the first few days. I wanted to bury my head in the sand and pretend it wasn't happening and that our time at Tyler's was just an extension of our weekend away. Eventually though, I had to face reality, speak to the police again and call my sister.

I sweep up the pieces of broken glass on the kitchen floor into a pile. I don't really know where else to start. There's stuff everywhere. Out of all the destruction and devastation Danny's left behind, the thing that hurts the most is the lost photographs and baby items that he's taken. Their baby photos can't be replaced, I don't have digital copies. I put off picking up the empty frames from the floor because it's too painful.

I wipe the stray tears away from my cheeks as I hear Chloe come in. Immediately she runs at me, wrapping her arms around me in a bear hug.

"Oh, Mandy!"

I hug my sister and cry into her sweatshirt. She gives me time to let it all out and doesn't rush my ugly crying session.

When I'm finally done, Chloe steps back and puts her hands on her hips, assessing the situation.

"Geez, he did a real number. Fucking bastard. I thought we were rid of this douchebag and then he does a thing like this!"

I sniff and blow my nose into a tissue, nodding in agreement.

"Still, never mind. It's nothing a cup of tea and a dustpan and brush can't fix." *Ever the optimist.*

Chloe and I spend the next few hours getting the house back to normal. By the time we're done and the workmen have finished, you'd never know anything had happened on the face of things. *But I know.* I know that the pictures and baby memories are missing. I know that he's been here amongst our things. I know that this house will never feel the same again.

When we're finally finished, Chloe and I flop onto the sofa in an exhausted heap and I rest my head on her shoulder.

"I don't think I want to come home, Chlo."

Chloe gives my hand a sympathetic squeeze. "I'm not surprised now that you're living at Mr Fancypants' mansion," she teases.

"It's not that." I chuckle.

"I know, I'm only teasing. Have you told him how you feel?"

"No. I don't want him to think I'm after his money or taking advantage. He only just said 'I love you', it's a bit of a leap to ask to move me and my two kids in permanently."

"Not necessarily. How do you know he's not secretly wishing you'd stay?" she shrugs.

I don't reply, I just sit quietly mulling over what she said as I pick at the edge of the sofa cushion.

"Talk to him, Mandy." Chloe nudges me with her shoulder, making me smile.

"I'll talk to him tonight."

"That a girl. Now let's get some food. I'm starving after all that cleaning."

I'm just about to move my aching legs off the sofa when my phone starts to ring. It's the school's number.

"Hello?" I answer.

"Miss Wells it's the secretary. I need you to come to the school right away. There's a situation at the gate with Ruby and Ronan. There's a man here."

"What do you mean a man?" I don't know why I'm asking, I know exactly who it is. My stomach flips over multiple times making me feel nauseous. "Where is Tyler?" I ask hurriedly, not even giving her a chance to reply to the first question.

"He's with them. Please hurry Miss Wells."

"I'm on my way. Have the police been called?" I ask, frantically searching for my car keys.

"Yes, they're on their way too."

I cut the call without even saying goodbye or thank you, my brain is too busy firing off in a million different directions.

"Danny's at the school," I tell Chloe, finally finding my car keys under the coffee table. "I need to get there."

"Let me drive. You're not thinking straight."

I don't argue, I just toss her the keys as we head out the front door. I try calling Tyler's mobile but it rings and rings before going to answerphone.

Please pick up. I can't let him take my children.

Chapter Twenty-Seven

Tyler

Whatever's going on out here, it's escalating fast. The crowd of students that has gathered at the gate is enormous. I still can't see through it yet to see exactly what's happening. I feel sick to my stomach as I sprint across the playground to the commotion.

"Excuse me," I boom loudly, trying to fight my way through the sea of students. "You need to step aside."

Eventually, I navigate my way through the hordes of nosey bystanders and reach the front of the crowd, only to be met with a sickening scene. Ruby is standing at the front, her face is red and blotchy as if she's been crying for some time. Her friends are attempting to shield her from the man who's yelling at her from where he's standing beside his beat-up car. A man who I assume is Danny. He looks a bit like the twins except that his eyes are wild, I'd almost certainly say he's under the influence of something. His hair is a mess of dark curls and he looks as if he hasn't washed for some time. There are stains down the front of his t-shirt and he's missing several teeth.

"Ruby, hurry up and get your arse in this car," he hollers. He can't even stand up straight, he's swaying about all over the place.

"You're Ruby's father, I assume?" I try to keep my voice casual in an attempt to calm the situation down.

"What the fuck's it got to do with you?" He spits the words angrily at me like they taste bad.

"Rather a lot actually. I'm the Headteacher and I'm going to need to ask you to remove yourself from the premises immediately."

If circumstances were different and I wasn't at work in front of all these students, there's so much I'd like to say to this low-life piece of shit, but instead, I'm forced to be professional and squash my thoughts.

"Oh fuck off. I've come to get my daughter. It's got naught to do with you."

Ruby looks at me in sheer terror. I give her a reassuring smile as she clutches her friend's arm.

"That won't be happening, I'm afraid. I cannot release Ruby into your care while you're under the influence. Especially not if you plan on driving your car."

The noise of the crowd of students behind me is almost deafening. *Where are the backup staff I asked for?*

"Go on, deck him Mr Woodgate!" I hear one of the boys yell. "Yeah, knock him out!"

I ignore the ridiculous heckling behind me and focus on Danny. He's unpredictable and I need to get this situation under control before someone gets hurt.

"You can't stop me, she's my kid. Who the fuck are you to tell me I can't have my own kid?" He sneers at me, swaying on the spot. It's a wonder he hasn't fallen flat on his face yet.

He turns his attention back to Ruby, "Will you hurry up! I haven't got all day. Where's your brother? Tell him to hurry the fuck up too."

"I'm not going with you," Ruby sobs, shrinking further into her group of friends.

"You'll do as your fucking told!" He screams. Clearly no is a word that Danny doesn't like and he's losing his cool that he's not getting his way.

Danny marches forward towards Ruby and lunges at her, sending the girls into a screaming frenzy. I block his path by standing between them but it's enough for the crowd of students to descend into chaos. The situation goes from bad to worse as the students start to push and shove each other all yelling over one another and becoming hysterical.

Squaring up to me, Danny gets right in my face and shoves me hard in the chest, making me stumble backwards into the students.

"Fight! Fight! Fight!" They all start to chant.

"Are you alright, Ruby?" I ask her, regaining my footing. I deliberately ignore the arsehole in front of me. *He can wait.*

"I'm scared!" She cries. "I don't want to go with him."

"You're not going anywhere." I reassure her. Over my dead body he is taking her.

"I don't have time for this shit!" Danny roars, coming at me again. "Get in the fucking car Ruby!"

I step towards him to stop him getting any closer to Ruby and he takes a swing at me, punching me square in the face. This time I fall back, unable to stop myself and land on a few of the older boys who help me up.

My jaw stings like a bitch as I wipe my lip. I can feel the blood trickling down my chin. More gasps and screams emanate from the students. Luckily none of them have been stupid enough to get involved or try to take him on themselves.

Staggering to my feet, a handful of teachers arrive on the scene looking panic stricken.

"Get the students back." I instruct them, ignoring their horrified faces.

Just as the other teachers start to usher then backwards away from Danny, Ronan arrives, bursting his way through the crowds to get to Ruby.

"Ruby!" He calls, finding her at the front with her friends. He then notices my smashed up face and spots his dad staggering about beside me. "What the fuck?" Ronan mutters under his breath.

"There's my boy!" Danny shouts, louder than is necessary. "Come on son, we're leaving."

"Like hell we are." Ronan fires back. "What are you doing here, Dad? What have you done to Ty-Mr Woodgate?"

"I'm here to pick you up. Take you out for something nice and show you my new place." Danny slurs his words. He can't even stand in one place without moving or swaying.

"Dad, you're drunk or high. Get lost. No one wants you here. Look at how upset Ruby is."

"She always was a cry baby, I blame your mother for the way she turned out," he sneers.

I can predict Ronan's reaction before it happens. I grab him round the chest from behind and hold his arms down, stopping him from flying at Danny.

"What did you fucking say?" He shouts at Danny.

"Ronan, don't. He's not worth it." I growl in his ear as I try to keep hold of him. He's strong though, it takes everything I've got to hold him back.

"Ooh you grew up feisty!" Danny grins, poking fun at his enraged son. "There's hope for you yet. At least you're not a complete pussy like your teacher here."

Ronan unleashes a string of profanities at Danny and fights against me to let him go but I hold onto him with all my strength. If I let him go, who knows what might happen.

"Let me go!" He hisses at me through gritted teeth. "I'm going to kill him!"

I'm momentarily distracted when I spot Amanda's car pulling up across the street. Ronan takes advantage of my split-second lapse in focus and breaks free from my arms, charging forward towards Danny. Despite his inebriated state, Danny's reflexes are lightning fast and he grabs hold of Ruby by the throat and drags her in front of him, producing a pen knife from his pocket.

Everyone screams in horror and Ruby holds her breath, her terrified eyes as wide as saucers as she shakes against Danny and his blade.

Ronan holds his hands up backing off out of fear for Ruby. *Fuck. Fuck. Fuck.* That all unravelled so fast.

Amanda runs across the street towards us, screaming. The sound of her screams alerts Danny to her presence and he shuffles himself and Ruby round to face her.

"Hello Mandy, nice of you to join us," he grins like a maniac. *He truly is the devil.*

Chapter Twenty-Eight

Amanda

I thought I'd felt fear before in my life but I've never known the true meaning until this moment. Being able to see the whites of Ruby's eyes from halfway across the street as she shakes in terror is fear on a level I didn't think possible. The scene I've walked into is far worse than anything I could have imagined. Ruby pleads silently with her eyes for me to do something. My eyes dart around the carnage and chaos, trying to process it all. Teachers are fighting to hold back tens of students, Tyler is bleeding and beaten as he holds Ronan's arm, begging him not to do anything stupid.

"Mum," Ruby whispers through her tears. She's too scared to even speak out loud, Danny's pen knife mere millimetres from her throat.

You often hear stories of people gaining superhuman strength from an adrenaline rush in times like these. I can believe that's true. I feel like I could tear through concrete with my bare hands right now if it'd save my little girl. Despite the raging inferno inside me, I have to be smart about this. One wrong move and Ruby's life could be over.

I glance over at Tyler who understands the need to handle this with care. I can't hear what he's saying but he's whispering in his ear, doing his best to keep Ronan calm.

"What are you doing, Danny?" I ask as calmly as I can manage. Terror is trying to claw its way up and out my throat but I won't let it. My daughter's life is at stake.

"I've come for my kids. You weren't listening to me Mandy so I'm here." His frantic eyes dart around wildly.

"Why now? What is this really about?"

"I want to see my kids. I miss them."

"Miss us?!" Ronan roars, fighting against the confines of Tyler's arms. "You don't even know us!"

"Daddy, please let me go," Ruby sobs.

"This isn't really about them, is it Danny? I'm going to guess that Natasha left you?"

I can instantly tell I've hit a nerve by his shift in body language. Natasha was his latest girlfriend, or victim, depending on how you look at it. I heard through friends they had separated.

"This isn't about that stupid slut! It's about my kids." Danny's grip on the knife ever so slightly loosens as he's becoming distracted by the direction this conversation has taken.

"No, Danny, it's about control. You've lost the power you had over someone else, *again*, and you're looking for a replacement."

"That's not true!" He spits.

As I talk, I'm subtly edging sideways in the hopes that Danny will keep facing me and end up with his back to Tyler and Ronan. It's a long shot as I can't tell them what I'm thinking, I just hope they see the same opportunity I do and act on it.

"You won't find what you're looking for with these two. They can't be controlled, Danny. They're teenagers, you can't bully and manipulate them. They're headstrong." None of these are bad traits in my children, I just need to keep him talking.

"I wonder where they learnt that," he sneers, looking down his crooked nose at me. There was a time when a comment like that from him would have hurt me deeply but now I see him for the pathetic excuse of a man that he is.

"Let her go, Danny. Please." I doubt there's any humanity left in there but it's worth a shot. I would do anything right now to get Ruby out of this situation.

"They're coming with me!" He snaps, pushing Ruby forward towards the car. Ruby cries harder and tries to resist. The fresh panic in her eyes obliterates my calm facade and I cry out.

"Stop it!" I beg.

Tyler takes the opportunity of Danny having his back to him and lunges forward knocking the pen knife out of his hand and it skids across the playground. Ronan grabs Ruby and pulls her out of harms way as Tyler tackles Danny to the ground and holds his arms behind his back. With his face crushed against the tarmac he growls and shouts at Tyler.

"You fucking bastard!"

I run to Ruby and Ronan and hold them both tightly as we crumple to a heap on the cold ground, sobbing in each other's arms.

The crowd of students, still being held back by the rest of the teachers, all cheer Tyler on as holds Danny down. A faint sound of police sirens start to be heard in the distance. *It's over.* The relief only makes me cry harder.

"I love you both so much," I tell them through my tears. "I'm so sorry."

Neither of them speaks, they hold on tightly to me and each other as they let out all of their pain and fear.

The police quickly take control of the situation and arrest Danny, bundling him into the back of the van as he kicks and spits at the officers. No children should ever have to witness what happened here today, let alone by one of their own parents. A lot of damage has been done and it will take the twins time to heal and recover, but we have each other and we have Tyler. As if he can sense that I'm thinking about him, Tyler looks over at me from where he's standing speaking to the police officers. He looks completely exhausted but relieved. The bruising on his poor face is already starting to show.

"Can I go and talk to Tyler?" Ronan asks, finally lifting his head from my shoulder.

"Of course you can," I answer softly, wiping a stray tear from his cheek. "Why don't we all go?"

The three of us get up off the floor and make our way over to Tyler. The crowd of students behind us is now dissipating as the officers and teachers dismiss them. I'm sure the police will want to take statements from them but everyone's been through enough for one day. Ruby lets go of my hand and runs towards Tyler, wrapping her arms around his waist, almost knocking him off his feet.

"Thank you," she cries into his shirt, squeezing him tight.

Just when I think I can't cry anymore or feel any more emotional than I already do, she goes and does a thing like that, making my heart melt into a puddle on the floor. Tyler wraps his arms around her and holds her as she cries. "You're going to be alright, kid."

Ronan holds his hand out for Tyler to shake. "Thank you," he says. "Who knows what would have happened without you."

Tyler nods, clearly struggling to deal with all the praise. He's not one to revel in the spotlight. An officer approaches us and addresses Tyler.

"Are you ready to come down to the station?"

"He won't be in any trouble will he?" Ronan asks the officer. "He saved my sister's life. He's a hero."

Tyler clears his throat uncomfortably.

"We just need to ask you all some questions, if that's ok. No one's in any trouble apart from your Dad."

"He's no dad." Ronan mutters.

"He won't be allowed near us again, will he?" Ruby looks up from Tyler's chest at the officer with big sad eyes.

"Absolutely not."

The ride to the station is quiet as everyone tries to process the day's events in their own exhausted way. Ruby sits beside Ronan, her head resting on his shoulder as they both doze in and out of sleep. Tyler is beside me with his hand firmly in mine, rubbing soothing circles across the back of my hand with his thumb.

"I can never repay you for what you did today," I whisper.

"Sshh. Don't even say another word. Anyone would have done the same."

"But anyone didn't. You did, and I love you so much for it."

Tyler looks at me, his tired face suddenly coming to life as we both realise what I've just said. I never envisaged telling him that for the first time in the back of a police car but then again nothing about us has ever really been very conventional. I've said it back to him before, but this is the first time it's come from me.

"I love you too, Amanda Wells."

Despite their eyes being closed, I'm sure I see the hint of a smile playing around the corners of Ruby's mouth.

Everything's going to be ok.

Chapter Twenty-Nine

Tyler

Fourteen months later...

"Ruby! Ronan! Come down!" Amanda calls up the stairs for what must be the fourth time this morning. "It's Christmas!"

Amanda is a vision of festive beauty in her deep red, crushed velvet dress. Her long wavy hair falls over her shoulders and she has matching red lipstick and sparkly eye makeup. Naturally, she has a pair of sexy as hell heels to go with her outfit. A brand new pair that she unwrapped from me this morning while we sipped Prosecco in bed. *Life is good.*

Spending Christmas at the Lake House is more perfect than I could have imagined. We even had a sprinkling of snow yesterday while we were out walking. Not that the twins appreciated it, they moaned relentlessly about the cold, the mud, the wind - pretty much everything! Having the opportunity to make new memories here to add to the old ones is a gift in itself.

The aroma of roast turkey wafts from the oven through the house in preparation of our guests arriving soon. How the smell alone hasn't got Ruby and Ronan out of bed is a mystery, it's mouth-watering!

"Why are they not up yet?" Amanda pouts at me in the most sexy way, making me want to bite her bottom lip.

"They're teenagers. Being excited about Christmas is against the rules." I chuckle, wrapping my arms around her waist. "I'm here though, and I'm excited. Why don't you help me roll the pastry for the mince pies while we wait?"

Amanda smiles and takes a step back, eyeing me up and down. "I do like you in that apron."

"If you're a good girl I'll show you what's underneath it later." I flash her a cheeky wink. Making her laugh.

"Yes, Sir," she giggles, swatting my arm as we walk towards the kitchen.

Half an hour later and the mince pies are in the oven, a new bottle of Prosecco has been popped and Christmas music is blaring through the house. I spin Amanda around, forcing her to dance with me in the kitchen as she laughs uncontrollably. Nothing makes me happier than the sound of their laughter filling the house. I'm so incredibly lucky that I get to call them my family.

Amanda bumps into the cupboard in her fit of giggles so I take the opportunity to press her up against it and steal a kiss. She tastes like peppermint from the candy cane she stole from the tree earlier. I run my hand across the soft material of her dress and fist the other one in her hair, ready to get all kinds of carried when we hear a groan from behind us.

"Put her down, seriously. I think I might puke." Ronan complains from the doorway with a smirk. His hair is all messed up from sleep and he's wearing nothing but a Santa hat and a pair of pyjama bottoms with the Grinch on. "Merry Christmas."

"Merry Christmas, darling!" Amanda squeals, escaping from me and dashing over to hug Ronan. He rolls his eyes but doesn't stop her. I'm learning fast that Amanda is an unstoppable force at Christmas, her enthusiasm is infectious.

Ruby appears too, bleary-eyed and yawning, wrapped up in a gingerbread blanket like some sort of festive sausage roll. *These kids.* They never fail to make me smile on a daily basis, even when they're being impossible.

Before we get any further, the doorbell rings and the front door swings open with a bang.

"Ho Ho Ho! Merry Christmas" My brother booms, making a spectacular entrance as per usual. The twins flock to him like bees around honey, they think he's hilarious, the big dumb goofball. He barrels in with armfuls of gifts and a huge smile, closely followed by Emily, who slides in quietly behind him. How these two work is a wonder, they couldn't be more different, but somehow they do. Chloe also arrives at the same time and the happy hubbub in the house is off the charts.

Amanda gets to work as the hostess with the mostest, taking everyone's coats and swapping them for drinks and nibbles. She's in her element rushing around with trays of smoked salmon and dip. There's certainly no danger of anyone going hungry today.

I sit back in the armchair with my beer, watching everything going on around me. We've come so far. I try not to think back to the day when Danny got arrested, it was a harrowing day for all involved, but to see everyone now and how happy they are is remarkably touching. It took a while to get here, the months that followed were hard. The twins struggled, each in their own way and Amanda suffered but we made it through. Ruby and Ronan saw the best counsellor money could buy and they've made real progress. I stepped down from my position as Executive Headteacher. It felt like the right decision given all that had gone on and I now work in an advisory role which means I'm around more to be there for my family. *My family.*

Amanda comes and sits herself on my knee whilst I'm deep in thought. "Everything ok?" she asks, popping a chocolate chip cookie in my mouth.

"Everything's perfect." I mumble around my mouthful. I try to smile but all the crumbs fall out of my mouth into my lap, making Amanda laugh.

"Someone get the old man a bib," Tom shouts, making Ronan double over with laughter. *Idiots.* Sometimes I regret introducing these two to each other, they're as thick as thieves.

"Don't let them get to you," Amanda whispers in my ear with a giggle. "You're the hottest old man I know and I can't wait to have you all to myself later."

I shift in my seat as Amanda subtly flicks her tongue over my earlobe. "Can't we just kick them all out now? I murmur back. "I have a bit of a growing situation that needs dealing with."

Amanda raises one eyebrow seductively. "No, you'll have to wait," she smirks."We haven't opened presents yet."

"That's what I'm trying to tell you. I have a huge one for you right here, ready to unwrap."

Amanda ignores me, rolling her eyes playfully and pulling me in for a kiss.

"Can you two be less cute please?" Chloe digs, walking into the room with a fresh glass of wine. "Some of us are single and bitter, you know."

"You'll find your person, Aunty Chloe." Ruby reassures her, "And if not you can get a whole bunch of cats."

The room erupts into laughter and Chloe sticks her tongue out like a child.

"Who's ready for some presents?" Amanda chirps, clapping her hands together in front of her in delight.

A lot of whooping and cheering breaks out around the room, which Amanda takes as a yes.

"Will you give me a hand dishing them out?"

Amanda and I get on our hands and knees at the foot of the Christmas tree to read the labels and hand out all the gifts. I dont think I've ever seen so many presents. There's a particularly special one with Amanda's name on it that I'm keeping a look out for so that I can give it to her at just the right moment. I keep handing out gifts as I hunt for it, the pile gradually getting smaller.

"Who's this for?" I call out, coming across a flat parcel with a tag that reads 'Dad,' on the front.

"It's for you," Ruby and Ronan both answer in unison.

A lump forms in my throat at the gesture. I can't believe they put that tag on it. Amanda squeezes my hand and gives me a twinkly-eyed smile. She must know about this. I look at the twins quizzically.

"I told you once that Danny didn't deserve the title of Dad. No one deserves it more than you do." Ronan says. "Open it."

I feel like I've been hit by a freight train. I clear my throat to try and keep my emotions at bay. The whole room is watching me as I process what Ruby and Ronan are saying and open their gift. Inside the wrapping is an envelope. I take some papers out from inside and turn them over so I can read what they are. I see the word 'adoption' across the top in big black letters and fall apart. My heart cracks wide open while I fight to keep the tears at bay.

"What do you say?" Ruby asks hopefully from across the room. She's clutching at Ronan's arm, waiting for my response.

"It would be an absolute honour." I manage to choke out.

Everyone claps and cheers and I'm certain I hear the sound of corks popping in the background. I sit in a dazed bubble on the floor beneath the Christmas tree letting it sink in. Ruby and Ronan rush over to me and bundle me onto the floor like a pair of excitable puppies.

"I thought you said it was against the rules for teenagers to be excited at Christmas?" Amanda jokes.

"What do I know?!" I laugh, my voice muffled from being buried beneath the twins.

I make a mental note to slip the gift I have for Amanda away for another day. Nothing can take away what the twins have asked of me today. This is about them and I want them to know how overwhelmed and happy I am that they want me to be their dad. My question can wait. We have the rest of our lives together as a family to figure out the rest.

Acknowledgements

I have wanted to write this book for so long, and now that I have, I can't believe it's over. I loved every minute of writing Tyler and Amanda's story. They've been living in my head with me for a very long time and I kind of miss them now that they've gone quiet. Writing this book coincided with a lot of difficulties in my own parenting journey and so it took a lot longer than I anticipated and was emotionally much harder to finish. If it weren't for all the amazingly supportive people around me and the unwavering belief of my readers, I'm not sure I would have got there this time!

A huge thank you needs to go out to my husband and children for putting up with me! My brain is a crazy place that's always busy and full of rapidly changing ideas. It must be like living with a hurricane! But they are always encouraging me to write and follow my dream.

I would also like to thank my beta readers, Claire and Pat. These wonderful ladies have also had a tough time recently, each in their own different ways, and yet they have both still found the time to listen to me and my crazy nonsense and help me through the writing process. I will forever be grateful for these two ladies in my life.

I am also lucky enough to have the most incredible ARC and street team, many of whom have been with me since the very first book. These ladies give me the best, honest feedback and help me to constantly grow as a writer. This is the kind of support that money can't buy, they are just genuinely lovely people.

Last but not least, I would also like to say a huge thank you to you for reading my book. Whether this is the first book of mine you've ever read, or simply the latest, thank you. It means the world to me that you took the time to buy or download and read my characters' stories.

More by B Crowhurst

Rock Your World
Head Over Heels
Kiss From a Rose (novella)
Honeymoon Heat (novella)

<u>The Paradise Hotel Stories</u>
Welcome to Paradise
Return to Paradise
Paradise Forever

https://www.amazon.co.uk/stores/B-Crowhurst/author/B08W6SG7SV